"Once I get my life in order, I'd like to look you up.

"I mean, if you want me to," Ash added.

The seconds before Maura nodded were torture. "I'd like that, very much." Ash's heart pounded in his chest.

Until he heard the masculine shout.

"Maura!"

An alarm went off.

He should have known better. Known that luck was not currency that could be hoarded and stored up until you really, really needed it—or really wanted it.

And oh, he'd wanted Maura! Ash had wanted her so much, he had drained his luck, just so he might have a chance with this woman. A chance at life. A chance at happiness.

Clearly, that was impossible now.

Not when the man coming toward them was one of the most powerful men in the county.

And not when he was Maura's father.

Unless…somehow, he could convince this woman that while he wasn't yet the man she believed him to be, he intended to become that man. Or die trying.

Dear Reader,

As you take a break from raking those autumn leaves, you'll want to check out our latest Silhouette Special Edition novels! This month, we're thrilled to feature Stella Bagwell's *Should Have Been Her Child* (#1570), the first book in her new miniseries, MEN OF THE WEST. Stella writes that this series is full of "rough, tough cowboys, the strong bond of sibling love and the wide-open skies of the west. Mix those elements with a dash of intrigue, mayhem and a whole lot of romance and you get the Ketchum family!" And we can't wait to read their stories!

Next, Christine Rimmer brings us *The Marriage Medallion* (#1567), the third book in her VIKING BRIDES series, which is all about matrimonial destiny and solving secrets of the past. In Jodi O'Donnell's *The Rancher's Daughter* (#1568), part of popular series MONTANA MAVERICKS: THE KINGSLEYS, two unlikely soul mates are trapped in a cave…and find a way to stay warm. *Practice Makes Pregnant* (#1569) by Lois Faye Dyer, the fourth book in the MANHATTAN MULTIPLES series, tells the story of a night of passion and a very unexpected development between a handsome attorney and a bashful assistant. Will their marriage of convenience turn to everlasting love?

Patricia Kay will hook readers into an intricate family dynamic and heart-thumping romance in *Secrets of a Small Town* (#1571). And Karen Sandler's *Counting on a Cowboy* (#1572) is an engaging tale about a good-hearted teacher who finds love with a rancher and his young daughter. You won't want to miss this touching story!

Stay warm in this crisp weather with six complex and satisfying romances. And be sure to return next month for more emotional storytelling from Silhouette Special Edition!

Happy reading!

Gail Chasan
Senior Editor

Please address questions and book requests to:
Silhouette Reader Service
U.S.: 3010 Walden Ave., P.O. Box 1325, Buffalo, NY 14269
Canadian: P.O. Box 609, Fort Erie, Ont. L2A 5X3

The Rancher's Daughter

JODI O'DONNELL

SPECIAL EDITION™

Published by Silhouette Books

America's Publisher of Contemporary Romance

Special thanks and acknowledgment are given to
Jodi O'Donnell for her contribution to the
MONTANA MAVERICKS series.

For Carol and Cindy, for keeping me laughing

SILHOUETTE BOOKS

ISBN 0-373-24568-8

THE RANCHER'S DAUGHTER

Visit Silhouette at www.eHarlequin.com

Printed in U.S.A.

Books by Jodi O'Donnell

Silhouette Special Edition

Of Texas Ladies, Cowboys...and Babies #1045
Cowboy Boots and Glasss Slippers #1284
When Baby Was Born #1339
*The Come-Back Cowboy #1494
The Rancher's Daughter #1568

Silhouette Romance

Still Sweet on Him #969
The Farmer Takes a Wife #992
A Man To Remember #1021
Daddy Was a Cowboy #1080
Real Marriage Material #1213
Dr. Dad to the Rescue #1385
*The Rancher's Promise #1619
*His Best Friend's Bride #1625

*Bridgewater Bachelors

JODI O'DONNELL

grew up one of fourteen children in small-town Iowa. As a result, she loves to explore in her writing how family relationships influence who and why we love as we do.

A *USA TODAY* bestselling author, Jodi has also been a finalist for the Romance Writers of America's RITA® Award, and is a past winner of RWA's Golden Heart Award. She lives in Iowa with her two dogs, Rio and Leia.

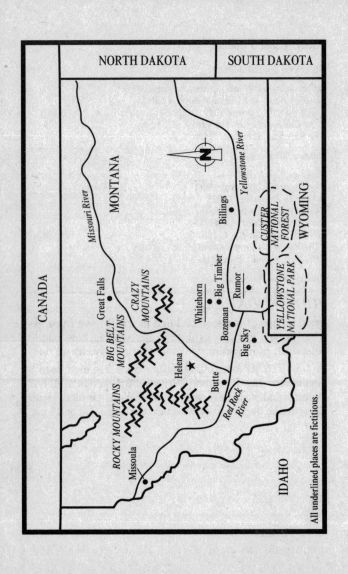

All underlined places are fictitious.

Chapter One

"It's a blowup! Run!"

The shout was like a shotgun blast in Maura Kingsley's ears. She didn't even hesitate. Without turning to see who'd issued the order—she knew, anyway, that it was Hal Chatsworth, the boss of her crew of firefighters—Maura took off in a sprint across the pine-studded steppe and away from the forest fire that the national media had recently dubbed the worst in Montana's history.

Her ax-hoe-hybrid Pulaski clutched in her right hand, she dashed through the bone-dry forest duff, dodging ponderosa pines that were as drought-stressed as Maura had ever seen in her three years with the Forest Service. She was aware of her crewmates, as well as others who'd been on the burnout detail, running toward the good black in the riverbed that Hal had designated a safety zone at the beginning of the shift, should the winds change direction.

There was no predicting when a fire might achieve the critical mass it needed to reinforce itself with its own heat and instantly incinerating flames, creating the vicious vortex called a firestorm. The only way to fight that kind of fire was to get out of its way.

The problem was, Maura realized as a crackling branch fell to earth in front of her, the fire was crowning above their heads, leaping from treetop to treetop at a pace faster than the firefighters were running. Embers rained down on her like the sparks of a firecracker as she picked up her pace.

Good heavens, but it was moving fast. Too fast for her to outrun.

She could feel its heat, like the draft from a blast furnace, on her back. Gasping for breath as she ran, she clutched the pouch on her belt as if it were a talisman. It contained the collapsible fiberglass and aluminum fire shelter that would be her only chance of survival should she truly become overcome by the flames licking at the heels of her lug-soled boots. It was a firefighter's worst nightmare, getting caught in a burnover, where the white-hot heat of a raging wildfire could reach over 1,000 degrees Fahrenheit.

Not for the first time in her life Maura prayed for a little height and longer legs as she felt herself falling behind the others. Her goggles obscuring her peripheral vision, she turned her head from side to side, trying to get an idea of what her options might be. To her right was only more sparsely treed forest, to her left the craggy limestone face of a rock mountain. Neither left her much to choose from. In fact, she'd be in ten times worse trouble heading for the mountainside if the flames chose to follow her. A fire moved faster up a slope because the uphill fuels became preheated.

She'd have to do something, though, and quick. The wind whipped around her, scaring up more sparks. She could almost taste more than smell the acrid, black smoke. It burned in her throat like a draft of home-stilled whiskey, and as she ran, she tugged the protective mask around her neck over her mouth and nose.

It was the noise, however, that started panic rising in her chest. Even from half a mile away, a forest fire sounded like a tornado, jumbo jet and fifty-car pileup all rolled into one. This close, it was the very incarnation of chaos and destruction. She had a wild thought that, like surviving a deadly battle, one couldn't completely understand the sound of a forest fire without experiencing it firsthand.

If she survived, for abruptly she was not in front of the fire. It was around her, ahead of her, above her.

And the realization hit Maura in an avalanche: She was not going to make it out.

Her life fast-forwarded past her mind's eye: her childhood growing up on a ranch, good times with her family—her three older brothers who alternately teased her unmercifully and pampered her unstintingly. Her mother, so regal and refined. Carolyn Kingsley was like a rose growing out of wild and rugged Montana grassland, and Maura had always been puzzled by the difference between mother and daughter, for she herself was of that land as much as it was of her.

Like her father, Stratton. Headstrong, loving, imperious, tender. She'd spent her life trying to thwart his protectiveness.

There was no way he could protect her now.

Around her, trees were literally exploding where they were rooted. The sound was like so many dying screams for mercy.

With a choking cry, Maura made the agonizing decision to pull out her fire shelter and take refuge under it. Survival using the shelter was not a certainty. One breath of superheated air would kill her, if she didn't die of sheer terror before the fire passed over her. But it was her only hope.

Then, just as she slowed, her heart like a melon in her throat, Maura felt herself swept forward from behind.

"Come on," a masculine voice rasped into her ear. "There's got to be cover along that mountain slope that'll be safer than out in the open under nothin' but a flimsy tent."

She hadn't the presence of mind—or desire—to argue as the man, a fellow firefighter, although she didn't know exactly who, cut to the left at an angle, half carrying her. Her feet glanced the ground as she ran beside him, the black canvas fire pack containing her water bottles, rations and other essential supplies bouncing against her lower back. Her own effort was nearly useless; his long strides ate up territory as if he himself was the fire and wind rolled into one.

They reached the face of the mountain in less than a minute. Barely slowing his pace, he groped feverishly with the gloved hand of his free arm at the outcroppings, overhangs and ledges in the craggy gray limestone.

''There's got to be some kind of decent shelter here, damn it!'' he shouted over the roar of the wildfire. She dared a moment's pause to shoot a glance at him and could see only grim eyes behind his goggles, his own fire mask and yellow helmet obscuring any other features.

The ground was rougher here, punctuated with rocks and boulders surrounded by sprigs of parched wheat- and needlegrass. In college, she'd studied the geology of every major forest and mountain range in Montana and knew he was right. Caves were not unusual in this kind of sedimentary rock. But who knew where one might appear or if it would be deep enough to provide adequate shelter from the fire?

Perspiration from the exertion, heat and fear ran in rivulets down every vertical plane of her body. Her eyes smarting from the smoke, Maura's gaze searched the mountainside as desperately as that of the firefighter who'd come to her rescue. Maybe he hadn't rescued her, though. Maybe he'd sealed his death warrant by coming to her aid.

For the fire had again caught up to them, and here, along the slope, there was no place to go to escape it.

Her legs like jelly, Maura tripped over a rock and stumbled to her knees, and he lost his grip on her waist.

''Leave me!'' she gasped when he turned back to her. ''Save yourself.''

He said nothing, just grabbed her by her upper arm and yanked her up. She staggered to her feet and against his side.

As soon as she did, a flaming fifty-foot-tall pine came crashing down behind them, directly across the spot where she'd knelt a second before. Maura screamed reflexively as the firefighter shoved her behind him, protecting her from the billow of sparks with his own body. She fell again, this time backward into a clump of bone-dry sagebrush sprouting horizontally from the mountain's side. But she didn't stop there; she continued falling, plunging through the shrubbery. She cracked the back of her helmet on the ground and for a moment believed she'd lost consciousness when everything went dim. Then Maura realized that, miraculously, she was lying at the lip of a cave.

She sobbed her relief. "A ca—" Her cry was cut off by a cough that felt as if she'd dislodged a piece of lung. Maura struggled to sit up and batted madly at the prickly dry sagebrush to part it. Sucking in a desperate breath, she shouted, "It's a cave!"

But the firefighter had already comprehended her discovery. He reached down to give her a boost to her feet, then led the way into the dark, unknown interior of the cave, pausing only to flick on the headlamp strapped to the front of his helmet.

The difference in temperature and noise was day and night. Still sucking air through a raw windpipe and smarting where she'd jarred her head, Maura turned on her own headlamp and, although she could see not much more than the back of the firefighter's head and shoulders, she knew they'd lucked out. *She'd* lucked out for the second time in only a few precious minutes, the first being this man's rescue of her.

Now that she was out of the thick of it, the closeness

of the tragedy they'd both barely escaped dropped full-blown on her consciousness like a cougar from a tree.

"Wait!" she gasped, slumping against the rough wall and tugging her mask down to draw in a much-needed draught of cool air.

The man stopped and turned. "What's the holdup?" he asked tersely.

She lifted her forearm to shade her eyes from the beam of his headlamp. It didn't help. She could see nothing, just the bright, white light. Coming out of the encompassing blackness behind him, the glow seemed otherworldly, and it set her nerves jangling even more.

"We almost got killed out there!" Her voice wobbled revealingly. "I...just need a moment to catch my b-breath."

"Really." There was a moment of silence, then he said, "I know this fire is some kind of wicked, but I didn't think the NIFC was so desperate for bodies to fight it they'd started letting powder puffs onto Type Two crews."

That got her spine straightening, as well as adding a precious half inch to her five-foot-two height. "I passed the work capacity pack test, just like everyone else, hiking three miles in forty-five minutes carrying a forty-five-pound payload." She drew in another breath. "I made it with time to spare, too, I'll have you know! And I held my own on both the Deadwood and Durango fires last year."

He cocked his head to one side, sending his headlamp's beam in another direction and out of her eyes, and she got an impression of sardonic eyes a color she still couldn't make out.

"Really," he repeated, and this time the word was loaded with skepticism. "Then this oughta be a piece of cake."

And he headed farther into the mountain again, with Maura, now more vexed than scared, scrambling to keep up.

Powder puff, indeed! She supposed he had some right to be annoyed at having to come to her rescue, but some aspects of firefighting had not so much to do with speed and strength and everything to do with intuition and luck.

The passage was narrow and low, but navigable. The cave floor sloped gently downward, and very quickly became wet and slick, as did the walls striated in golds and reds and browns.

They had gone what Maura estimated to be about a hundred feet when the cave opened up into a large chamber. Its ceiling rose ten feet above them, and she simply stood there flat-footed and openmouthed as her headlamp made a sweep of the rock formations: glowing yellow stalactites jutted from the ceiling like jagged sharks' teeth. The walls were both smoother and rougher looking than in the passageway, with humps of smooth flowstone and ragged "popcorn," the cauliflower-shaped clusters on the cave walls that she knew could be sharp as coral.

Though she'd studied caves in college, she'd never been much of a spelunker, and the sight of this one took her breath away.

"It's beautiful," she breathed, her recent fear receding as quickly as the heat, noise and threat of the fire had in the cool confines of the cave. It had the still, musty smell of condensation and earth, which was just fine with Maura, since any air movement might bring the smoke into the cave and suffocate them. Mingled with the smell was a pungency she knew had to be coming from the guano that littered the cave floor.

"Bats," she guessed aloud. They were notorious cave dwellers, along with other wild animals.

The man noted the direction of her gaze and nodded. "It's also our home, at least for the night," he said, tugging off his gloves and tucking them into his belt. He removed his own face mask and goggles, letting them dangle around his neck.

Undoing the straps to his fire pack, he examined the cave room with a much more critical eye. "It looks like it goes on, who knows how much deeper into the mountain. I'll take a look in a sec. Are you injured at all?"

"Incredibly, no. My throat is sandpapery from inhaling some smoke, but otherwise I'm fine." She felt for her eyebrows and found them both intact. They were usually the first to go.

"Good," the man said. "One less thing to have to worry about."

He removed his helmet, headlamp still on, and balanced it on a ledge about shoulder height, so that it lit the interior of the room. "Better take a reckoning of water and supplies."

As she divested herself of her own pack, Maura seized the opportunity to get a good look at her rescuer. He looked vaguely familiar, but then everyone did after a few weeks working on a firefighting crew, even with volunteers being trucked in from across the nation. He

was as sooty and begrimed as she was, his face blackened around the outline of his goggles in a kind of
reverse raccoon look. He was wearing the same Forest-
Service-issue brown fire-retardant Nomex pants and
yellow fire shirt, which he was absently unbuttoning,
but the uniform looked different on him than others.
His shoulders seemed uncommonly broad, his forearms, as he rolled up the long sleeves of his shirt, were
muscular, his hands wide and competent looking. He
appeared the very definition of an able-bodied man, she
thought, as her gaze lifted to his face again, and she
was confronted with his as-thorough scrutiny of her. It
was only then that she noticed his eyes: gray, they
were. Almost silver, only richer. They were remote and
inviting at once, and she was equally torn in two directions gazing into them. Afraid yet fascinated.

He was right in that they would be spending at least
the night here together. Neither of them had radios to
call for help, and even if they had, there would have
been no way to pick up a frequency this deep in the
mountain—or any way that rescue crews could get to
them at this point, with the fire still going full force
outside.

That wouldn't stop the rest of her crew and their
boss, Hal, from worrying about her, as would this
man's crew worry about him. News of their disappearance would go all the way to the command of the
National Interagency Fire Commission. She hoped they
wouldn't notify her family that she was missing. The
thought of her family's concern and fear for her made
her eyes sting with tears.

I'm fine, she telepathed to them. I'm safe in a cave

with the firefighter who saved my life. I couldn't be in better hands.

"I haven't thanked you for rescuing me," Maura said aloud, cursing the shakiness in her voice. She was battling a bout of nausea from the smoke. "I mean, I was ready to use my fire shelter, but I've heard firefighters say they'd rather spend a month in solitary confinement than an hour in a burnover."

"Really." His eyebrows lowered in sudden ferocity. "Well, as you pointed out, you're a trained firefighter. So it stands to reason you'd'd've done what you needed to do to survive." He'd finished unbuttoning his fire shirt, revealing the perspiration-stained T-shirt beneath, and now yanked its tail from his waistband with what occurred to her to be undue force. "Or am I wrong there, powder puff?"

"I certainly hope that, had you not come along, I would have done as I was trained," she said with crisp enunciation. "I was simply conveying my thanks."

She lifted her chin in Carolynesque regality. It was becoming difficult to be nice to this man, but she was determined to, precisely for the reason that he *had* saved her life. Still, she wasn't about to let him get away with the jibe about her size and gender.

"And you can stop calling me powder puff any time now," she warned mildly.

One corner of his mouth lifted almost in amusement as he looked her up and down, all five feet and two inches of her. But he said gamely enough, "All right. What's your name, then?"

"Maura. Maura King—"

A rustle coming from one of the openings that led

deeper into the cave interrupted her. The man, whose name remained a mystery to her, grabbed his helmet as he headed without hesitation down the passageway. The other animals, aside from bats, that might have taken refuge in the cave—grizzlies, cougars and wolverines among them—had Maura snatching up her own helmet to follow him, her boots slipping in the loose rock on the cave floor. She wasn't afraid; it might turn out that he would need *her* help this time.

So closely was she following him that she came up against his solid back when he stopped short several yards into the tunnel.

"What is it?" she asked.

"Shh," he admonished with a half turn of his head. He was hunched over in this part of the cave, which had a clearance closer to her height.

Curious, Maura peeked past his shoulder to see what had brought him up short: a young deer—it couldn't have been more than a month old—and an adult mule deer that had to be its mother, lying on her side.

The doe barely lifted her head at the sound of the intruders, and Maura realized she must be injured badly.

In a trice she'd stepped around the man and knelt beside the deer. The fawn's tiny hooves scrabbled in the dirt as it startled backward on stick legs.

"It's okay, little one," Maura soothed. She sat very still, waiting for the fawn to calm. She used the time to turn her headlamp upon the doe for a visual examination.

She was no veterinarian, but it didn't look good. The deer had suffered third-degree burns in places, the fur along its side, back and haunches singed a ruddy black. The animal's eyes were wide with fear, her breath was coming in short, labored bursts, nostrils flaring in distress and pain.

Maura swallowed back the lump that rose to her throat. "You're okay," she soothed. But she knew that, indeed, the doe was not okay.

The fawn, which stood quivering a few yards away, startled again when the man dropped to a crouch beside her.

"Looks pretty grim, doesn't it?" he said softly.

She set her mouth firmly. "We've got some options for making her comfortable."

He glanced sideways at her, doubt infusing every inch of his face. "You got a horse-size dose of pain-killer somewhere in your fire pack? 'Cause that's what it'll take."

She cocked her head to one side. "No, but do you hear that?"

He listened, and obviously detected what she had—trickling water coming from around the curve in the passage.

"An underground spring. The water's coolness will help ease the pain of the doe's burns, and drinking it will keep her hydrated," the man said with a nod toward both deer.

"How to get her to it, though?" Maura watched the rapid rise and fall of the doe's chest. "I mean, I've got a bottle of water in my pack but it's full and we'll need it ourselves. Still, even if I had an empty container to fetch water for her, she can't lift her head to drink."

He glanced about as if hoping to spy a solution within the confines of the cave. Then, in one fluid movement, he stood and shrugged out of his yellow fire shirt, then peeled off the T-shirt beneath it.

Maura tried not to stare. In the glow of light bouncing off the cave walls, every muscle of his arms, shoulders, chest and torso were as if carved in stone, like a Michelangelo statue.

And as perfectly built.

"Wh-what are you doing?" she croaked.

"Unless you've got a better idea, I'm going to soak this T-shirt in the spring, then trickle water into the doe's mouth as I wring it out."

She smiled. "It's a simple solution, but it'll probably work as well as any," she admitted.

He disappeared around the curve of the tunnel, and when he returned he had the sopping T-shirt in his palm. He knelt again and held the shirt over the doe's head. Squeezing gently, he dribbled water into her mouth. At first too frightened by the sensation to do anything but blow the water out with puffs of air, the doe quickly caught on and was soon lapping spasmodically at the droplets her rescuer continued to aim into her mouth.

He was concentrating on dribbling water into the doe's mouth, so Maura gave in to the fascination of watching him. As powerful as the strength was in those hands of his, there was also a gentleness that moved her to tears.

So engrossed was she in the process, it took Maura a few moments to realize what his comment of "Looks like someone else is thirsty" meant. The fawn had toddled a few tentative steps closer, nose, ears and body quivering in simultaneous need and fear.

"Here," she said, cupping her palms under the trickle of water until she had collected a few ounces. Walking slowly forward on her knees, she held out her offering to the baby.

He skittered back two steps. His eyes were huge and dark.

"Come on, Smokey," she cooed, spontaneously naming the youngster after the famous bear cub. "Don't be frightened. You've got nothing to be scared of. See how Mama's drinking? Why don't you take a drink, too."

His ears alternating between pricked forward in curiosity and flattened back in fear, the fawn was a study in the contradictory urges of doubt and trust. Maura wondered madly what reassurance to give him so he would take those last few steps toward her.

"Okay, so maybe you do have a few things to be scared of," she said softly. "There's a big, mean fire out there. Your mama's pretty sick, and you don't have a clue what's going to happen to her...or to you."

She extended her cupped hands an inch more. The fawn quivered like an aspen. From the corner of her eye, she was aware that her companion had stilled his movements so as not to frighten the fawn. Aware that he watched her with interest.

"I'm here now, though, along with this guy here," she murmured, tipping her head slightly in his direction. "He saved my hide, and that was not without some doin'. I just met him, but I've got the feeling he'll take care of you, too, just like he's helping your mama.'' Another inch forward. ''We'll get out of this, Smokey, I promise. But we've gotta stick together, okay?''

The fawn still had not moved, and the animal seemed to teeter on a precipice of indecision that had to be worse than his thirst. It tore Maura's heart.

''Take a drink, sweetie, please,'' she whispered. ''Trust me—trust yourself, too—and take a drink.''

The velvet brown eyes grew larger, the black nose trembled. Then the fawn took a tentative step toward her. Maura remained motionless, her arms and shoulders aching with the effort. She knew she could depend upon the firefighter remaining still, but if the doe showed any signs of agitation right now, that would be it for gaining the fawn's trust.

She met the animal's eyes unwaveringly.

And then he took another step, then another, before stretching his neck forward—and taking a tiny lap at the water in her palm. His nose tickled, yet Maura twitched not a muscle. He drank all that she had to offer, then toddled backward and sank down next to his mother.

Relieved and happy, Maura let her arms drop to her lap.

''You got some kind of sweet-talkin' ability there,'' the firefighter said quietly.

''Which has its merits…and its faults,'' she said pensively.

''What do you mean?''

The fawn had begun licking his mother's ear in his own offering of comfort. ''I had quite a bit of contact with wildlife during my fieldwork in the forestry pro-

gram at the University of Montana," Maura answered.
"I learned then that animals *should* be afraid of us
humans. We've done nothing to earn their trust. We've
ruined their home, rather than taken care of it for them.
The Rumor fire is proof positive of that. When it comes
down to it, that's why I became a volunteer firefighter.
I know the NIFC is still investigating how the Rumor
fire got started, but it's pretty clear it was a person—"

"And so it's only fitting that we humans risk our
lives to stop it," he finished for her.

"Right. And if we're able to save even one of the
thousands of animals who'll die before it's contained
for good—" she lifted her chin a notch in defiance
"—then I'm glad to have taken the risk."

To her dismay, she found herself fighting tears yet
again.

"Maura."

She took her gaze off the fawn to look at him. Those
gray eyes of his virtually glowed, fascinating her. How
could a shade one normally thought of as cool and
remote be so vibrant and compelling?

"Okay, so maybe there *is* a place for powder puffs
on a major fire," he murmured with such respect—
albeit somewhat grudging—that she forgot to chafe under the nickname.

Yes, her fascination for him was strong. But so was
her fear as his gaze dropped to her mouth in a movement that was blatantly erotic.

Maura had a sudden urge to scamper backward with
as much wariness as the fawn. She didn't, though, just
lifted her chin and asked tartly, "So what's *your*
name—unless you want me to make up some offensive
nickname to call you?"

Chapter Two

Maura's question, oh-so-innocently posed, brought him up short. A thousand emotions assailed him in that brief moment—sharp regret, shame and dread foremost among them. But this woman wouldn't know, didn't need to know, his entire history.

He drew in a calming breath, then answered succinctly. "Ash."

"Ash?" Maura repeated inanely.

"Short for Ashton. It's an old family name." He didn't offer his last name, and he knew Maura had to be wondering why. It was firefighter etiquette, especially when crews were being called in from all over the nation, to lead off with your full name, where you hailed from, how long you'd been firefighting and how long on this particular fire. It gave you a sense of your own time and place in the life of the fire.

But he had an aversion to volunteering too much information, developed over ten years of hard lessons. Brutal lessons.

Still, he found himself muttering, "Been a volunteer firefighter for the past five years, mostly in Montana and Idaho. This is my first week on this fire."

He grabbed his T-shirt and rose to his feet. "I'll go soak this in water again and bathe the doe's burns as best I can. There's not much else we can do."

If Maura was puzzled by the abrupt change of subject, she didn't show it. She bit her lower lip in thought, which only made her look ten times more earnest—and naive—than she already did. And ten times as irresistible.

He couldn't believe she was old enough to have graduated college, much less have been in the Forest Service long enough to work a couple of big fires. She barely came up to his shoulder, and with that schoolgirlish braid of red hair trailing over her shoulder and those innocent blue eyes, he'd have guessed her age closer to sixteen than twenty-something.

Except for when she stretched behind her for her helmet and one had a glimpse of the curve of a full, womanly breast and nipped-in waist.

She set the helmet so its headlamp shed better light onto the doe's injuries. "I'll take the first turn at bathing her burns, if you like. If we keep it up through the night, it'll ease her discomfort until we can get her proper veterinary care, don't you think?"

Ash simply stared at her. She had to know the animal wouldn't make it to morning. He wasn't going to clarify the point, however, not when Maura was looking up at him with her big blue eyes as if he could turn the world on its axis.

"Why not, I guess," Ash said, curbing the cynicism in his voice. "Let me take first crack at it, though, while you set up camp in the chamber where we left our gear."

She smiled, and it was like the sun breaking over the horizon. "Thanks, Ash."

She disappeared down the passage while Ash soaked and resoaked the T-shirt, being careful not to touch the doe's burns with it as he ran water over them. Her breathing did seem less labored, but that might be because she was barely clinging to life. He gave her another drink of water and tried to coax the fawn into taking one and failed.

Of course, ministering to the downtrodden and discouraged was Maura's specialty. That and her seemingly unrelenting optimism.

Ash sat back on his heels. *Optimism.* Now there was a word he'd long forgotten the meaning of. And a state of mind he hadn't been able to revive in himself since…well, since forever, it seemed.

But today he'd experienced the whiff of a remembrance, like a familiar scent from childhood drifting on the wind, of a time when he hadn't been skeptical of every hope that lifted its wings being dashed to pieces when it inevitably fell to earth. A time when every small taste of sweetness didn't come with a castor-oil dose of bitterness. A time when he wasn't constantly wary, could be open with his heart and know how to keep another's heart in trust.

And he supposed he had Maura to thank for that—

or should he curse her instead? Because she had only underscored how difficult, if not hopeless, was his journey toward redemption. Toward regaining such trust, in others as well as in himself.

With a shake of his head, Ash roused himself from his contemplation. Well, he only had to make it through the night with Maura and her hopefulness. And kindness. And honesty. And tantalizing appeal. He could keep her at a distance until the morning. Then, with any luck, he could say goodbye and return to reality.

Placing his hands on his thighs, Ash hauled himself to his feet and went to see how he could help her.

Maura glanced around as Ash entered the chamber, where she'd made inroads to getting organized for the night.

His gray eyes turned abruptly stormy as they took in the results of her efforts.

"What the hell is this?" he asked.

"I discovered the space blanket in your fire pack," she explained. "I laid it out next to the one I had, you know, so we could share our b-body heat." She couldn't believe she was stammering and blushing like a girl. "It'll help us keep warm."

"Really," Ash said in that one-word commentary she was coming to learn had a lot of different meanings. Such as right now, with how he'd slipped his fire shirt back on but hadn't buttoned it, as if oblivious to the cool temperature in the cave. He was also back to being remote, it seemed, and she wondered why.

"I also have a bunch of water purification tabs in

case we need to go that route," she prattled on almost nervously, "but with a combined total of four bottles of water, we should be good for a few days, if needed. And we both have compasses, duct tape and first aid kits, as well as some pretty complete rations."

She spread her hands, indicating the food she'd assembled on their space blankets. "Your three power bars along with my MRE," she said, referring to the ready-made meals that were available for firefighters to take with them when it seemed likely they might not make it back to fire camp that night.

"An MRE, huh?" He picked up the retort pouch the meal had come in and scrutinized it as if it were vermin. "'Hearty Beef Stew.' The problem is, it could say chicken or pasta or veggie delight on here, and it wouldn't matter. It all has the taste and texture of corrugated cardboard."

"How on earth did you get to be such a sourpuss!" she finally burst out, half teasing, half serious. "I think we can count ourselves lucky to have any kind of nourishment at all. And that we're in here, relatively safe and sound, instead of being the ones getting eaten alive by that fire out there!"

He looked at her strangely for a long moment, then shrugged. "You're right. Let's eat."

They settled into their spare meal, Maura sitting cross-legged across from Ash, who was doing the same. After her previous nausea, she was surprised to find herself as hungry as a bear, and it was difficult not to bolt her food. The MRE had come with a helping of apple crisp, and despite Ash's dearth of expectations, the dessert tasted as close to ambrosia as Maura could imagine.

Ash ate methodically and without enthusiasm, as if in the past he had indeed had to eat corrugated cardboard and like it. She couldn't help but be curious about his history, but she had a feeling they weren't going to pass the evening chummily sharing their life stories. Although it *would* be nice to know his last name, for crying out loud.

She was about to ask when he said, "It's true, you know."

"What is?" Maura asked.

"That the fire is alive. That it has a purpose. That it's vengeful. And it will swallow you up, just like the whale did Jonah."

She glanced sharply at him, wondering again at this change of mood. "You can't think about it that way. You know that. That's one of the first rules of firefighting. You make the fire too real and you lose your ability to combat it. And it'll consume you."

"Exactly." He continued eating methodically, musingly. "Either you're consumed with combating it, or it'll consume you. Either way, you lose something of yourself."

Was he right? Maura asked herself. Her thoughts turned to the fire that had been scorching the countryside for more than eight weeks since it started just outside of her hometown of Rumor. It had steadily marched, like a plague of locusts, south-southeast into the Custer National Forest, one of the most diverse and spectacular pieces of forestland in the state of Montana. Already the fire had torched more than 250,000 acres, leaving nothing in its wake, the soil charred so badly it was as hard as her plastic helmet.

And the fire didn't seem to be letting up. It *did* seem possessed, in fact, with its own vicious temper and capricious moods that were as unpredictable as that of a wild man, making the damage it did that much more senseless.

Maura set her dessert aside, no longer hungry. "Maybe you're right," she admitted. "But even if I try to be objective about forest fires, the truth is, I wouldn't be here if I didn't care about a lot of things having to do with the land."

She gave a rueful shake of her head. "It's the main reason I got a degree in forestry and natural resources management, because I love this state—love it like it's a part of me. This fire…well, you know how it goes. Its effects will reverberate throughout the whole eco-system. The jackrabbits, sage grouse and ground squir-rels lose food, shelter and nesting cover with the cheat-grass and sagebrush gone. With those animals dying off, there's nothing for raptors and snakes to prey on. And it goes on and on from there."

"It's called survival of the fittest," Ash murmured. He had set his meal aside, too. The dank, depressing smell in the cave seemed worse all of a sudden.

"Is it? Or is it not getting the God-given right to thrive and have a normal existence, like Smokey and his mother?"

He gazed at her calmly. "No one's ever said that life was fair."

She gestured around her, rather urgently, she realized. "And we're not to try and do our best to make it a little more fair?"

Was she trying to convince Ash? Or herself? She only knew she had to try.

She leaned forward intently, forearms on her knees. "You know how you have dreams you want so badly to make happen you can nearly taste it?"

"I guess." He was wary, watching her.

"Well, I have a dream. Someday I want to have a ranch. It wouldn't have to be big, maybe just a few dozen acres. I'd invite all kinds of disadvantaged children there—children from broken homes, or who've had some behavioral problems, or who just need a place to go after school instead of a dark, empty house." She clasped her hands in front of her. "I'd teach them how they can be a part of taking care of the land. I'd show them how we need to be good stewards and protect and preserve our environment and wildlife. And maybe by doing that, the children will learn how to be responsible and helpful and purposeful. And they'll feel safe and secure themselves. And happy."

"You think that will do it?" Ash asked. His voice wasn't skeptical so much as carefully neutral. "Spending some time on your ranch is gonna turn these kids' lives around, and it won't matter what they have to go back home to each evening?"

"I think it will help, at least a little, or maybe just enough." She dropped her chin, studying the sooty toes of her lug-soled boots. "I get frustrated, though, knowing that there are so many children and animals who are going without that help every day, every single day.''

She gave a huff of frustration, and again she couldn't have said with whom she was frustrated.

''You can't save the world, Maura,'' Ash said, and it was now as if he were trying to convince *her* of something that meant a great deal to him.

She wouldn't go there. She couldn't go there.

''If I help rescue just one soul,'' Maura said stubbornly, ''it'd be worth it. I mean, don't you feel your life has been given new purpose by saving mine?''

He didn't answer, only gazed at her with that same wariness.

She rose, needing to move, and went to stand at the entrance to the passage that led to the outside. Even from several yards in, the sound of the wind was like getting up close and personal with a volcano. The worst of the fire would have passed by now, but the danger—and the fury—were not over. They would never be over, for there would always be forest fires. There would always be the suffering of the innocent. It was a law of nature.

Panic again fought its way upward in her chest.

Distracting herself, Maura passed a palm across the back of her neck. ''Heavens, I feel grubby. I'd give anything for a nice hot shower.''

''I'd suggest freshening up in the spring,'' Ash said from behind her, ''but it's just a little spit of water, and the pool it flows into isn't something you'd give your dog a bath in, much less yourself.''

She turned to regard him. He had exhibited little reaction to her diatribe, except for his eyes returning

to that cool silver that created enough distance between
them you could have inserted the Grand Canyon with
room to spare. She knew she hadn't changed his mind
a bit. Of course, she knew what he believed; he'd said
it outright.

"Just a spit of water, eh?" She elevated her chin an
inch. "Not exactly my idea of clean, but better than
nothing."

She found the bar of Ivory she always kept in her
pack and took it and her helmet with her as she headed
stalwartly down the tunnel. She wasn't going to let Ash
Whatever-his-last-name-was get her down.

She gave the doe a quick check on the way by.
Smokey was still glued to his mother's side. Maura
stooped to soothe a hand down the bridge of the doe's
nose. She barely responded. She seemed to be resting
better, though. Maura would take the next turn bathing
the burns after her own abbreviated ablution.

The spring, she discovered, was the trifling affair
Ash had warned it would be, barely a trickle down the
side of one wall into a small muddy pool at the bottom.
She sighed. It would have to do.

Wedging her helmet into a crevice in the opposite
wall, she removed her fire shirt, then hesitated with her
hands on the hem of her T-shirt, listening. The only
sounds were that of the spring echoing in the chamber.
Not that Ash would peek; she knew that without asking. She drew the T-shirt over her head, reveling in the
feel of fresh, albeit cold, air on her skin, and impul-
sively removed her bra as well. She used the red bandanna she'd had tied around her throat to catch the
meager stream from the spring, soaped the dampened

area and washed herself as best she could, shivering a little in the cool of the cave. Meager as it was, the bath did revive her spirit.

She didn't know why she cared, anyway—about what Ash thought or if he had the disposition of a badger and an outlook so gloomy it would take a trip to the far side of the sun to brighten it up a bit. But she had to wonder what had made him that way: wary, secretive, cynical.

Something flitted past her ear, ruffling her hair. Maura knew it was a bat—she knew it—but she couldn't stifle a startled cry.

She gave another when barely three seconds later Ash appeared around the corner, his Pulaski gripped in his hand, his eyes wide with concern, his features taut. His stance that of knight ready to do battle.

Except that there was nothing to do battle with. And that's when Maura realized why, actually, his expression was so strained: Ash's headlamp had zeroed in like a spotlight on her naked torso. She felt like Gypsy Rose Lee on stage at the burlesque.

Maura gave yet another screech, this one of embarrassment, as she stooped, fumbling for her fire shirt to cover herself.

Realizing where the beam of his headlamp was trained, Ash whipped his helmet off his head and shoved it under his arm with military precision, so that the light now fell in a pool at his feet.

"Are you okay?" he asked belatedly. He had obviously been ready to come to her rescue for the second time that day. It wasn't the fact that she was standing there virtually half-naked that a thrill of goose bumps swept over her.

It was immediately followed by a thoroughly warming blush at the spark that leaped to his eyes, remote no more.

"A...a bat startled me," Maura stammered, clutching her shirt at her throat with one hand while holding it spread over her breasts with the other. "I'm fine...just embarrassed, is all. That I screamed, I mean, and made you come running. I must have scared the life out of *you*."

He finally averted his eyes, obviously nearly as embarrassed as she was.

"I didn't know if—or what—had happened." He actually shuffled his feet. "You know, if you'd seen a spider or if there was some kind of animal you'd come across that was threatening you..."

He shoved a hand through his dark hair. "Oh, hell."

Maura broke out into a smile. How sweet of him, just when she was about to give up on him. As much as he might pretend he was a hard case, she had a feeling Ash might be in the same league of softie as her father.

"I'm fine," Maura said, suddenly lighthearted, where a few moments ago she'd been ready to throw in the towel. "Really. I'm used to spiders and bats and most everything else. But thank you for coming to my rescue—again."

He mumbled something not quite sounding like "You're welcome," and stormed back down the passage without so much as a by-your-leave.

Maura's smile only widened. He couldn't have

seemed more uncomfortable than if she'd caught him in a lie.

And maybe she had.

Ash stalked—as best as one could hunched over and boot soles slip-sliding on a damp, uneven cave floor—back to the chamber where he and Maura had set up camp. Once there, he drew in half a dozen bracing breaths through clenched teeth.

He needed to get a grip on himself. He was taking this rescue business way too far. Maura was no shrinking violet who needed him to stomp on bugs or chase away critters. That had been clear from the start. It had been the whole point of calling her a powder puff. She had a degree in forestry, for Pete's sake, had probably spent more time braving the wilds of Montana than he had.

But, damn, it felt good to have her look at him with those big, blue eyes as if he was her own personal hero. And damn, but seeing her standing there, her skin wet and glowing, that red braid of hair, itself alive as the fire outside, spilling over one breast—it had been like glimpsing heaven.

A heaven he didn't even dare dream about.

And tonight was going to be hell, confined here in this cave with her. Ash swore, vividly and succinctly. He would almost rather have fought a thousand forest fires.

He looked around as he heard her return to the chamber.

"I can't tell you how much better I feel," she said cheerily and without a bit of her earlier embarrassment.

He had to admire her gumption. But then, she hadn't heard his next bit of news.

"Well, if you're done for the night, I'm thinkin' we'd better get some sleep." More brusquely than he meant to, he continued, "It's best if we shut off the headlamps to conserve our batteries. Chances are we'll make it out tomorrow, but we've actually got no idea how long we might have to hole up here before we can get out or someone else can get in."

He paused, then decided he might as well give it to her straight. "Once we turn out the light, it'll be black as six feet under in here, just to let you know. It could be kind of spooky."

She looked at him strangely before nodding. "I'll be fine."

"Then I'll let you get settled."

He headed back down to the spring for his own quick swab off. Ten minutes later he came back to find her on her side, her back to him, her space blanket wrapped around her, with her hard hat for a pillow. The small mound she made lying there looked not much bigger than a bag of feed.

Well, he may as well get this over with.

He dropped to his own space blanket. "Ready for me to turn off the headlamp?" Ash asked without preamble.

"Yes—oh, wait," Maura said, pushing back the blanket and half sitting up. "I forgot to take my turn at bathing the doe's burns."

Making a show of rustling around to get comfortable, he mumbled, "You don't have to. I...I checked on her while I was washing up."

"How is she doing?"

This was the worst news of all, and he'd have given his right arm not to have to tell it to her. But he owed her the truth.

"Maura, she died," Ash said.

Her eyes widened in shock, then closed as her mouth tightened into a thin line.

He felt like a twenty-four-carat louse. "It's for the best, you know," he said tersely. "She never did have a chance."

"I guess." Her head bent and she said nothing for a long moment. "And the fawn?"

"He seems to be doing fine, but he's not budging from her side." He paused, then added, "We won't leave him here. We'll get him out with us somehow."

She lifted her chin, and the watery smile she treated him to was so grateful it had him regretting his momentary weakness.

"So, you ready for me to turn out the light?" he said.

At her nod, Ash switched off his headlamp. Maura gave a soft gasp of surprise, and even he was momentarily taken aback. The darkness was absolute and enveloping. It was difficult to ignore it. Difficult to keep it at bay.

He distracted himself by experimenting with a more comfortable way to rest his head than on his helmet, and finally settled on using his bent arm. Either way, however, was about as conducive to sleep as trying to bunk in a herd of stampeding cattle. The space blanket had the flexibility of sheet metal and it crackled every time he breathed, but there wasn't any other choice for warmth.

He'd known it was chilly in the cave, but lying still without cover other than his clothes and the space blanket, and with the overwhelming darkness, it was like being shut up in a meat locker.

And nightmarishly reminiscent of another time in his life, when the darkness had been as complete, almost in danger of permeating his skin, like being submerged in a vat of blackest ink, until he became the darkness itself.

Ash shuddered. With effort, he concentrated on the sounds of the cave—the trickle of water, the soft whir of bat wings, the faint but ominous crackle and pop of the dying fire…a muffled sniff, and then another.

"Maura?" Ash said. "Are you okay?"

"Y-yes," came the muffled answer. There was no sound for a prolonged moment—and then a sob that sounded as if it had come bursting out of her like a cork from a bottle.

He fumbled for his headlamp and flicked it back on. Blinking to get his eyes adjusted, he was able to make out Maura huddled on her space blanket with her back to him.

"Maura, what's wrong?"

"Oh, no," she said. "I'm not going to tell you and have you call me powder puff and make some pithy comment about how real firefighters don't cry about the loss of wildlife and forest. After all, it's just p-part of the job, right? A part of life. No need to get all maudlin and teary-eyed."

"I wouldn't say those things," he denied rather sourly. "I mean, I know you've got a low opinion of me—one I haven't taken a lot of pains to discourage— but I'm not a complete hard-ass."

"And I am not a powder puff! Just because I believe in things turning out for the best and that I can have an impact on them, doesn't make me a lightweight or a Pollyanna or whatever you choose to call me."

She gave a flounce, but the effect was lost in a cellophane-like crinkling. "Maybe *you* believe I shouldn't have even tried to save that poor animal, or tried to ease her pain or her little one's fears. Just leave them alone and let nature take its course! Maybe you should have done that when you came up on me struggling to get out of the fire!"

"I don't believe that, and I wouldn't have let you get burnt to a crisp," Ash protested. But he could see he wouldn't change her mind that way. And he wanted to change her mind, he realized.

He took a deep breath, doubting what he was doing even as he was about to do it. "Just like I wouldn't let you lie over there crying without any comfort. So come here."

And without asking, he reached an arm around her waist to scoop her against him and hold her soft, small body against his.

Miracle of miracles, she turned into him as she sobbed against his shoulder. And miracle of miracles, it felt damned good—oh, not that it was good she was in such distress. But that he had even a prayer, simply by providing that shoulder, of easing her sorrow and pain.

It was a feeling he'd never experienced before. And he liked it a lot.

"What makes you think other firefighters aren't as torn up inside at the destruction they're witness to?" he asked once the storm of weeping seemed to abate.

"Oh, I don't think that about other firefighters." She sniffled. "Just you."

"I see." He hadn't exactly been a font of compassion, had he? "Well, actually, I fight fires because I have to. Like you, I can't sit by and watch this land go up in smoke. I…I love it too much."

"I knew that you did." Her voice wasn't triumphant, just quietly matter-of-fact. "Then why do you try to make people believe different?"

"I don't try to make people believe different," he said in echo of her own assertion. "Just you."

He was certainly treading on dangerous ground, now. But he didn't have to tell her how he'd gotten into volunteering to fight fires—that, indeed, he'd had a need to help out, but he'd also had a need to get out. Get out of the four walls that confined him, if only for a little while.

But that time—and those reasons—seemed of little significance at the moment. What counted was now, with Maura in his arms. Needing him in a way he hadn't let himself be needed in a decade.

She actually snuggled against him, and his arm tightened almost reflexively to bring her closer still. She was so small, so delicately built, he found himself marveling at the determination it must have taken for her to pass the physical test to qualify to be a firefighter. He had no doubt that she would achieve her dream of running a ranch for kids who needed a guiding hand. No doubt that somehow, some way, she would save that one soul that would make any amount of pain or disappointment worth it to her.

How he himself could have used that kind of support! His life might have turned out much differently....

"You know, I've kind of nourished a small dream myself," Ash said. He could barely believe he was speaking these words aloud—he'd mulled them over in his mind, certainly, millions of times—and yet he couldn't have stopped himself even if the hounds of hell were nipping at his heels. "A dream of owning a spread, too."

"You have?" He couldn't see her face, but her tone was encouraging.

"Yeah. In the past five years I've worked on a bunch of ranches from here to the Canadian border. That's how I got ranching in my blood. I'm foreman of a ranch right now—temporary foreman, that is, although it could turn into something long-term. Working in the role every day, knowing the herd better and better, along with every section they're grazing... It's only made me hunger for a place of my own, where I can look out across a herd and know every one of those cows is mine—mine to tend and raise up—and that the land they're standing on is well taken care of."

"It sounds like the ranch I want to have for disadvantaged children." Maura shifted to look up at him, and the movement brushed her breast against his ribs. He had to concentrate with all his might to temper his physical response. "I want them to learn about the land, how to think of the world beyond themselves."

He didn't want to put a damper on her enthusiasm, especially when it seemed he might have been able to turn her attitude about him a notch toward the positive, but he felt compelled to be honest with her. "It may be hard to do that, though, when their world is filled·

to the brim with worries about survival—where the next meal's coming from, how they'll stay warm at night. How they can ever feel safe and secure.''

He touched two fingers to her lips, forestalling her protest. ''I'm not tryin' to discourage you from following your dream, Maura. It's just that some kids struggle with a lot of problems that have to be addressed before they can even begin to think of others.''

I know that from experience, he thought but didn't say. *That* definitely was a subject for a whole different time.

Yet Maura must have gleaned enough information from his advice to guess. Gently she pulled his hand away. ''It must be a terrible, terrible thing to feel there's no one in the world you can count on. And I know that I don't have that kind of experience to help me relate to kids like that, Ash.''

She lifted her arm and, in a move that shocked him with its intimacy and power, she placed her palm on the side of his face, her thumb caressing his cheekbone. ''But I do know what it is like to feel safe…as safe as I feel in your arms right now, as if nothing can hurt me as long as I'm here. It's a wonderful feeling to give someone, too, even if you haven't felt it yourself.''

It floored him—that she felt safe with him. Secure. Despite everything.

''You don't even know me, Maura,'' Ash felt duty bound to warn her. ''You don't know.''

''Oh, I think I do. What I don't understand is why you want people to believe the worst about you. Because I won't. I won't believe you're not a hopeful person, too. You wouldn't have dreams if you weren't hopeful.''

Ash couldn't speak. The air in the cave was filled with emotion, ripe with desire. Even in the indirect light from his headlamp, her eyes were the clearest, purest blue, the expression in them heartbreakingly untouched. He would have given anything, anything to assure her she was right. And at that moment he almost felt he *could* assure her that he'd make his dream come true. Make *her* dream come true.

He didn't know how he might make it happen for her, make it happen for them both. But it just might be possible—if they did it together.

"I can't say as I completely buy your reasoning, but you make a pretty convincing argument, powder puff," he said roughly.

She frowned engagingly. Adorably. Her lower lip pouted, and he knew just what he wanted to do with it. With her.

"Apparently I haven't convinced you how singularly unappealing I find that nickname to be," she said in that oh-so-proper manner he'd witnessed earlier that evening. He wondered where she'd picked it up, being as how she was as elemental as the fire outside.

"Really," Ash drawled. "'Cause I find it—and you—smack dab the opposite."

And he lowered his head to take her mouth with his.

Chapter Three

His kiss was wild, dangerous, incendiary.

Maura's first instinct was to pull back, push him away. She barely knew this man, had only learned his name a few hours ago; not to mention the fact that, even if he had saved her life, he exuded the kind of danger that could ruin it, too. He'd said as much. Had warned her.

But that was the Maura Kingsley who had always dealt with her father's protectiveness by going the extra mile to be responsible, to show she could handle independence by overachieving everything she endeavored.

Yet the woman who was responding to the slow, sweet suction of Ash's mouth on hers with a low moan, who inched her fingers up the hard planes of his chest as she'd been dying to do since the moment he'd removed his shirt—well, this was another Maura entirely. Oh, yes, he had a dark side. In her ignorance of such places in the soul, it frightened her. But the depth of emotion that lived in those places also fascinated her. And she wanted to know what it felt like to walk on the wild side with this man, if only for a little while.

He seemed perfectly willing to take her there as his mouth went on a slow, sensuous exploration of her jaw and throat and ear. Maura clutched Ash's shoulders in what was becoming a familiar sensation with him— pain-pleasure, danger-refuge, downfall-salvation. And when his head dipped lower, chin nuzzling aside the placket of her shirt so that his hot breath branded the tender skin of her breast, Maura reflexively arched her back, urging him on.

Yet he hesitated. "I want you, Maura," he rasped against her throat. "Heaven knows I want you. But…"

"But what?" she asked, tugging his head upward with her fingers in his hair so that she could look into his eyes, wanting to know, needing to know what tormented him, and not just about tonight.

His gaze was torn, verging on the remote, cool gray that made her feel so alone and the dangerously smoldering ashes that seemed only an instant from spontaneous combustion.

"But who knows what will happen after we leave here," he said. "I know it seems right at the moment— damn, it feels right—but I…I wouldn't be completely honest with you if I didn't tell you that I don't have the best record when it comes to things like…like being dependable—"

"Only in risking your own life to save another's, you mean," she interrupted stalwartly.

"I mean it, Maura. I've messed up royally in the past…and it's hurt the people I care about."

"You wouldn't be here fighting fires, though, if you didn't believe there was a chance at redemption," she said. She couldn't let him feel so bereft of hope—about the world, about people, about himself.

His gaze was still divided. "All I'm saying is, I've taken risks before that ended in disaster, and I won't have you involved in the fallout."

"You took a risk saving me that did work out, and I will never forget it, Ash." She pressed her palm against his cheek in emphasis, and he covered it with his own.

"Never?" he asked raggedly.

"Never," she whispered, tugging him close to seal her promise with a kiss that immediately turned to searing passion, like being in the center of the fire.

"Make love to me, Ash," Maura begged, and he did as she asked, undressing her slowly. Even though the air was chilly on her skin, he immediately warmed her body with his.

"You're beautiful, Maura," he murmured. His fingertips grazed her belly on their way upward along her rib cage and circling back to brush one knuckle across her nipple. Maura's gasp of pleasure was swallowed by his mouth on hers as he continued caressing first one breast and then the other, until she thought she would die.

She plucked at the buttons of his shirt, wanting him as naked as she, and he obliged with a disrobing that was feverish, made only more so by the soft kisses she delighted in placing across the hard planes of his chest, along the line of his jaw, throughout the sprinkling of hair leading to his navel. His hands and mouth on her were as thrilling, with the brush of his palm over her hip, the trail of his tongue over her nipple, the brush of his fingers up the inside of her thigh to touch her intimately.

"Please, Ash," she found herself pleading, half out of her mind. *"Please."*

He poised himself over her, and there was an agonizing moment of hesitation when Maura thought he might change his mind. And then he was suddenly, gloriously filling her, his groan of satisfaction echoing hers.

They moved as one, in perfect complement, in perfect understanding, and the sensation was like no other she'd ever experienced. It was as if he was giving her something quite rare, quite precious. More than her giving him her trust, he was bestowing his on her.

And as completion came to them both, she vowed she would never betray that trust. Never.

She felt as if she'd been waiting all her life for this moment, for this man, and she hadn't even known it until now. He was as elemental as the fire that had nearly devoured them; as the life-giving water used to abate the fiercest of thirsts; as the earth within which the two of them now lay, sheltered and secure.

And she slept the sleep of the trustful.

Ash lay wide awake, Maura tucked against his side. Together, they *were* warmer, but it was still a cool fifty-some degrees in the cave, so he'd slid back into his pants and fire shirt, and had gently eased a sleepy Maura into hers before settling her back against him.

He wondered, for the hundredth time in an hour, when he had earned the points to be allowed a moment like this. Somebody needed to give him a pinch.

He'd meant his warning about not being dependable more as a reminder to himself than for her. Still, he couldn't help but find himself looking toward tomorrow with more enthusiasm than he had a few hours ago.

She was exactly the kind of woman he'd secretly dreamed of making a life with. A woman who was down-to-earth and not afraid to get her hands dirty. A woman who loved the land and all the glory and heartache that came from giving one's soul to such a changeable, untamed being.

For unlike fire, the land *was* something to imbue with life. And how like this woman that land was. Mysterious, fascinating, captivating. Both strong and gentle, she was somehow capable, as he was not, to open her heart even in the face of terrible pain.

And that was what he needed most. He needed a woman whose hardy hopefulness set a balance against his own charred and blighted hope.

Ash gazed down at Maura, at her perfectly serene face. Oh, he had no illusions that she'd be able to inspire new growth in him—not quite. All the hope and love in the world would have a hard time doing that.

But maybe, just maybe, she would keep his spirit from turning completely to ashes.

*   *   *

Morning came, but not in the conventional sense of the word.

Ash opened his eyes to utter darkness, which sent his heart pounding before he remembered where he was and who lay tucked into the crook of his arm.

The headlamp on his helmet must have gone out in the middle of the night, and once he'd carefully untwined himself from Maura's sleeping form, he searched around for her helmet. He found it with a minimum of effort and flicked the light on, careful to aim it away from her. She stirred briefly before settling back into her sleep with a soft sigh.

Creaking to his feet, he shook out the kinks in his back and shoulders, then shivered all over like a dog. Damn, it was cold and damp in this place! He knew that what he would find outside would stand in stark contrast, and dreaded going there.

Slowly Ash made his way to the front of the cave, listening for any clue as to what he might find. He heard nothing.

Still, even having worked clean-up crew on half a dozen fires, he wasn't prepared for the utter devastation he encountered stepping out of the cave.

The entire landscape was charred black. Burned tree trunks lay scattered on the ground like spilled toothpicks. Smoke hung low over the ground, making it appear as if a ghostly mist shrouded the valley. But there was no mystery or moisture in this fog.

The worst was the sound—or lack of it. There was none of the usual noises of life in the forest: the call of birds or the scuffle of animals in the brush or even the rustle of leaves in the breeze. There was only the intermittent pop of dying embers.

He and Maura had come so close to losing their lives.

She was stirring when he returned, blinking and struggling to sit up as the beam again filled the chamber.

Ash glanced at his watch. "It's coming up on 6:00 a.m. I figure we can pack up and try making our way to the riverbed to see where the fire went from there. If it looks unpassable or like we're just putting ourselves in more danger, we'll come back here for another night and try our luck tomorrow. But we better make an effort to get back to camp, if at all possible, so we don't draw firefighters off the fire and maybe into danger trying to find us. If that plan suits you, I mean," he hastily amended.

He knew he was being brusque, which had to confuse the hell out of her, but he was deathly afraid of what he would—or wouldn't—see in her eyes.

"That sounds like a good approach. What about Smokey?"

He finally looked at her, and it was in exasperation. "I said we wouldn't leave him behind, and we won't. I keep my word."

"Of course you do, Ash," Maura said calmly. She met his gaze steadily, and it took him by surprise to see there all of what he'd glimpsed in her eyes last night, and more.

Relief came in a tidal wave. He gave a nod. "I'll fetch him just before we're ready to leave, then."

They packed quickly and efficiently, the way firefighters do, and once he'd strapped his pack on, Ash went to retrieve the fawn. He thought he'd have a struggle on his hands, but the little guy barely protested when Ash stooped to lift him in his arms, where the fawn rested his head wearily against Ash's biceps.

He hoped to heaven the youngster wasn't falling ill, too. It'd kill Maura to lose him as well as the doe.

He spared a glance at the doe's body. "She's not in pain anymore, Smoke," he murmured to the baby deer. He noticed that his throat constricted with a sudden anguish he wouldn't have let himself experience before last night. "Nothing can hurt her again. At least there's that comfort."

Once outside, he and Maura followed the edge of the slope for a few miles, looking for a way to climb up to a ridge so they could get an idea of where the fire had gone. They soon found a fairly easy grade that at least got them a hundred or so feet above the valley floor. Once there, Ash saw the impact of the fire in full detail.

The destruction went on as far as the eye could see. Acres and acres, miles and miles of nothing but devastation, as if a nuclear bomb had struck.

And still the fire burned. A plume of smoke rose over another ridge in the distance.

The day was already hot and dry. It was going to be another scorcher, in more ways than one.

He turned to Maura, whose face was white with shock.

"Oh, Ash!" she cried softly. Her eyes filled with tears.

He resisted the almost overwhelming urge to take

her in his arms and comfort her, first because he already carried an armful of baby deer, and second because he had no appreciation that such comfort would help all that much. Last night had been an escape from the world and all of its pain, he realized. He wouldn't trade that moment for anything, but it had only been temporary, fleeting. This was reality, and it was here to stay.

"It looks like the fire headed southwest," he said without inflection. "We should be good to head to fire camp about four miles up the riverbed, and from there we can get a ride to command in Limestone."

She swiped at her eyes, nodding.

The way was rough, part of it through still-smoldering debris, a dangerous route to take. One didn't know when a still-standing tree trunk might topple. At one point, they came upon an abandoned fire shelter, and Maura and Ash simply exchanged looks, not speaking. Hopefully the firefighter who'd employed the shelter had survived and was also making his or her way back to camp.

It took them all of the morning and into the early afternoon to reach fire camp, where they were greeted with hugs and slaps on the back, their return hailed a miracle, for when the wind had shifted and started the fire's deadly run, not every firefighter had been as lucky as Ash and Maura: two National Park Service firefighters had gotten caught on a slope and died.

Ash and Maura looked at each other solemnly. Yes, they had come close to dying. But they hadn't. Whether it'd been sheer luck or destiny, they'd survived.

They reported to the incident commander, who released them to return to Limestone on the next truck, and from there, home. Hal, Maura's crew chief, radioed ahead for a veterinarian to be in Limestone for the fawn.

It was just a little one-horse town, but to Ash, Limestone looked like paradise as the truck came to a stop in front of the mercantile that was being used as a command center for the NIFC. As he and Maura stepped onto the street, Ash found himself blurting out, "Maura, wait."

"Yes, Ash?"

Glancing around, he pulled her aside with his free arm. With the other he was still holding on to Smokey, who'd nearly panicked earlier when Ash had tried to put him down.

He found a spot behind the truck for privacy, and she stood before him, looking up at him expectantly. He wanted badly to make good on that expectancy.

"Look, before we go our separate ways, I wanted you to know that last night meant something to me. What that something is, I still haven't figured out yet." He actually found he could give a short laugh. "But I hope you'll give me your address—you know, I just realized I don't have a clue what part of Montana you're from—and once I take care of some old business, get my life in order, I'd like to look you up in a few months or so. I mean, if you want me to."

The few seconds before she nodded were torture. "I'd like that, very much." Her smile could make flowers bloom.

Ash's heart was pounding like a drum within his

chest. He could barely believe he was here, asking these things of her, promising some of them himself. "I still can't make you any guarantees, Maura."

"I know you'll do your best to give what you can." Her confidence meant everything to him.

He gave an answering nod. It *would* work out, some way. He'd make a name for himself managing the Holmes ranch and build up some savings, start scouting around for where he might be able to lease some grazing land, as a start. More important, he'd make peace with his family, put to rest the lingering demons that still haunted him. And then he'd be free to give Maura the kind of happiness she deserved. He had to borrow some of her hopefulness, enough to believe it was possible—

"Maura!" Ash heard a masculine shout.

They both turned, and striding toward them was a tall man in his sixties or so with a head of steel-gray hair. Although the relief wreathing his weathered features told of the recent fear he'd experienced, he walked with the air of a man used to being in command, used to being in control.

"Dad?" Maura said wonderingly, then with a cry of joy, "Dad!"

An alarm went off in Ash's brain, a warning of the self-preservation kind that he hadn't experienced since his days in the pen at Deer Lodge. His first reaction was to put his back to a wall, any wall, to protect it, so that any danger he had to confront would be in front of him; so that if he was going down, he'd have the best chance of taking at least one other with him.

But he was no longer a prisoner, not of that sort, at

least. And he wasn't in the position of being able to take out the opponent.

Not when that man was none other than Stratton Kingsley, one of the most powerful men in the county.

And not when he was Maura's father.

Maura was swept up in a powerful, rib-cracking embrace that left her gasping for breath and happy enough to walk on air.

"Dad! What're you doing here?" She pulled away to peer into his craggy, beloved face. It was a study in worry.

"The branch director at the BLM is an old friend of mine, and I've had him keepin' an eye on you ever since you took up this fool notion of firefighting. He called me at the ranch the minute you turned up missing."

Maura lifted her eyebrows, not entirely happy to hear this. "I should have known."

"Don't give me that look. I've had enough grief today." He drew her head back against his shoulder, and she could feel his Adam's apple bob. "I thought I'd lost you, little girl."

"Well, as you can see I'm right as rain, Dad," Maura chided, even though it was pure heaven to feel those familiar arms around her, hugging her so tight she was beginning to get dizzy. "And it's all on account of this man."

She extracted herself from her father's embrace to tug Ash forward by his elbow. "Ash here saved my life—and Smokey's, too. We wouldn't have made it without him, Dad."

Smiling, she glanced up at Ash's face, only to find his expression as stony as granite. He was staring at her father with eyes full of shock and suspicion. Puzzled, Maura turned to her father—only to find the same emotions shooting lightning bolts from his eyes.

"Dad? Ash? What is it?" she asked, alarmed.

"You?" Stratton said, his piercing green gaze, which Maura had seen many a man whither under in less than ten seconds, still riveted on Ash. "You're the firefighter my daughter was holed up with all night long?"

"That would be me," Ash said with deadly calm. He hadn't moved a muscle, but his skin had turned white under his five-o'clock shadow, and Maura wondered what could have made it so.

"If you've, by God, touched a hair on her head, I'll horsewhip you and leave you for the buzzards to pick over, you young outlaw," Stratton warned.

Maura gasped. "Dad! What on earth is wrong with you? Chances are I wouldn't be standing here if it weren't for Ash!"

She stepped between them, although she couldn't have said what impulse told her to do so. "Why are you acting this way toward the man who risked his life to save mine?"

Stratton jabbed a pointed finger in Ash's direction. "Did he tell you, then, who he is and just what kinds of risks with people's lives he's normally used to taking?"

"What?" Maura asked, thoroughly confused, except for the thin thread of a memory that spun its way through her head like a familiar melody that she couldn't quite identify the name of.

"You remember Emmeline McDonough, don't you, Maura?" her father went on. "She was in the grade ahead of you in school—till she got taken out when she was about thirteen and put in a foster home over in Big Timber. See, her mama'd died and there was no one to take care of her on account of her brother Karl fighting over in Desert Storm—"

"And her other brother being in prison, sent there on a drug conviction that disgraced the family and broke his mother's heart."

This had come from Ash.

He turned to face her at last, his face a mask even as he held his strong chin not aloft in defiance nor tucked in shame, but level, as would a man who'd come to terms with his faults and mistakes and was going on with his life.

Then she looked into his eyes and saw the real story. For they no longer glowed silver, as they had when he'd made tender, passionate love to her.

Ash's eyes instead were the dull gray of ashes, cold and lifeless.

"That's right, Maura," he said in as colorless a tone, "you're lookin' at none other than Ash McDonough— otherwise known as the bad seed of Rumor, Montana."

He should have known better. Known that luck was not currency that could be hoarded and stored up for a rainy day when you really, really needed it—or really, really wanted it.

And, oh, he'd wanted Maura! Ash had wanted her

so much he had drained his luck down to a zero balance, just so he could believe for one night that he might have a chance with this woman. A chance at life. A chance at happiness.

Clearly, that was impossible now.

Who'd have known that out of the hundreds and hundreds of firefighters from all over the country, the one he'd share such an encounter with would be from his own hometown, giving her ready access to every sordid detail of his past, like it was on loan at the library.

It wasn't as if he'd intended to keep his history a secret from Maura forever—just until he'd made it right and put it behind him for good. And even with her finding out about that past now, he might have had a chance of convincing any other woman that while he might not yet be the man she believed him to be, he intended to become that man or die trying.

But not Stratton Kingsley's "little girl."

How? How was he to know the unpretentious, gutsy, warm, accepting woman he'd spent the night with was a member of one of the wealthiest families in this part of Montana? The Kingsley ranch alone would have put them up in rarefied air, but they also owned MonMart, the superstore chain that was poised to give such giants as Wal-Mart a run for their money. There was even a Kingsley Avenue running smack-dab through the middle of Rumor!

There was no way he could convince Maura Kingsley—or her father—that he could make her happy.

So. He didn't have much choice now but to get through the next few minutes and go on with his life.

"I guess I'm not surprised to be treated like a no-account by you, Stratton, or anyone who's acquainted with my past," Ash drawled, getting a bit of his own back when the other man's eyes widened in anger at the use of his first name by Rumor's bad seed.

He shifted the fawn to the side, hiking the little guy on one hip and tucking him under his arm, thoroughly aware of how ludicrous he must look standing there holding Bambi. "Rest assured, though, that you've got nothing to worry about when it comes to compromising your daughter here. There's no reason for either of us to have anything to do with each other from here on out."

Maura's face filled with confusion. "But, Ash, you just said you wanted for us to—"

"I said a lot of things, Maura," he cut her off. He couldn't stand for Stratton to hear his most private of desires. "But you'll remember the one I kept repeating was that I couldn't make you any guarantees."

He saw the shock in her eyes at his harsh tone, and he hated himself for it. But it was best to make this quick and final. She'd thank him some day.

"We both've got to live in the same town, and contrary to what your dad here is thinkin', I don't want any trouble," Ash went on. "Sure, I'm still on parole for a few more months, but I paid my dues and now I'm back to make amends to family and build a respectable life for myself. I don't want any trouble," he repeated, and hoped he didn't sound as desperate to Maura and her father as he did to himself. "And from *my* point of view, you're exactly that."

He steeled himself against the hurt and confusion he saw in her eyes. He couldn't let it get to him, let her get to him. It was too much of a risk, and he'd risked enough already. And lost.

Not trusting himself to utter another word, Ash gave a short nod in lieu of goodbye and walked away, the little fawn still tucked under one arm.

Maura turned on her father like a fury.

"How could you, Dad?" she exclaimed. "Ash saved my *life!*"

He had the grace to look abashed. "Fine. I owe him my eternal thanks for that. But that doesn't mean *you* need to."

He actually shook his index finger at her. "And you know what I mean. I don't need a damned crystal ball to know what happened in that cave last night. I don't care if he did snatch you from the jaws of death, he's no gentleman to take advantage of you that way."

Maura set her hands on her hips. "I can't believe you! I wasn't exactly coerced, you know."

At her implication, Stratton looked about to burst a blood vessel, his face was so red. Still, he didn't continue his tirade.

Maura sighed. Her father's lung cancer had been in remission for five years, but she didn't need to do anything to aggravate him right back into it. Why, though, was he treating her as if she were a teenager who got picked up by the sheriff for parking out by Lake Monet?

But Maura knew the answer to that. Her father had always been overprotective of her, seeing as how she was both the youngest and the only girl. For that matter, *all* of her brothers—from Russell to Reed to Tag and even her cousin Jeff, normally reasonable men all—had a blind spot when it came to her. She'd spent a major portion of her life trying to get out from under the protective wing they sheltered her with, which was doubly difficult when one stopped growing at slightly over five feet.

She hadn't let it or them stop her, however. She'd graduated a full two years early from high school and gone straight into the forestry program in Missoula. There, she'd signed up for the toughest assignments and was the first in line to take the firefighting test when she was old enough.

She had never let anything, physical or psychological, stand in the way of her doing what she wanted.

Maura gazed at Stratton lovingly. There were other considerations, however, that she had always taken into account, her father's love and concern for her foremost among them. She had never purposefully worried her parents, had always made sure they knew that she was well prepared for the challenges she might undertake and was prudent in carrying them out. When she took this approach, usually both Stratton and Carolyn came around, even if they still weren't completely happy with her decisions.

She had a feeling, though, that Ash McDonough was not a risk her father would ever see clear to condone.

Rumor's bad seed. She cringed inwardly. How Ash must have suffered under that nickname! And she could only imagine the circumstances that had led to his being saddled with it. She seemed to remember something about a drug bust and the scandal it caused around town, but she'd been only twelve or so and would have been protected from learning the details of such sordid business by her parents.

Even without the details, though, she knew Ash was somehow not the bad seed people portrayed him as. She knew it.

But how to prove it to her father—and perhaps to Ash himself?

"You're acting this way, Dad, because you don't know Ash," Maura said, hoping to make some progress right now.

"And after less than twenty-four hours you do?" Stratton asked, green eyes skeptical.

"Yes, I believe I do. He's got a strong code of honor about taking care of those less fortunate and making the world a better place. He's got a strong love of the land." Another quality struck her as she stood there. "He judges people on the merit of what they do and how they act—and not how big their ranches are or how much money they have in the bank."

She looked at him guilelessly. "And isn't that how you and Mom brought me up to think?"

Stratton's expression softened. "Of course that's how we brought up all of you kids. And you're a credit to us in everything you do. But can't you see it my way? Ash McDonough did hard time for selling drugs. Doesn't *that* tell you he's not a man of honor?"

Her certainty faltered for a moment, then rallied as she recalled how she'd felt in Ash's arms. "Not at all. He made a mistake and, like he said, he paid his dues. He's not afraid to admit he was wrong, and now he's here to make it up to those who had to suffer on account of his mistake. I find that pretty admirable."

She knew she shouldn't say what was on the tip of her tongue, but her father's mouth was as set as a piece of petrified wood.

"You should, too," she said, "because he's a lot like you."

Stratton's face turned that apoplectic red again. Well then, so be it. Maura was willing to risk stirring up her father's sensibilities even if it stirred up his blood pressure as well. He needed to find some reasonableness where she was concerned.

Clearly, though, that wasn't going to come without some strife.

"You're not to see him again, Maura," Stratton said in no uncertain terms. "You *don't* know Ash McDonough and you're not going to get to know him."

"But—"

"No buts about it. I'm your father and you're still living under my roof. Am I clear?"

This time Maura didn't try to argue but simply smiled. "You're perfectly clear, Dad."

"I mean it—" He broke off, peering at her suspiciously. "All right then," he said with a decisive nod. "Now, let's get you home so your mother can have her turn hugging the life out of you and threatening to end it if you scare either of us like that again."

"Yes, Dad," Maura said, perfectly willing to go along—for now.

Oh, he was clear, all right. That didn't mean she was going to do what her father said. She was twenty-two, with a mind of her own.

And that mind—and heart and body—wanted Ash McDonough in the worst way.

Chapter Four

"More, uh...more coffee?"

Ash glanced up from his breakfast at the teenage waitress standing next to his table. She looked as if she would rather take tea with the devil than serve coffee to the notorious Ash McDonough. Just fifteen minutes ago she'd nearly dumped his Chubby Checker—which was nothing more than a gimmicky name for three eggs, half a dozen slices of bacon and a mound of hash browns—in his lap when serving him, so he felt justified eyeing the pot of hot coffee she held with the same wariness she'd bestowed on him.

"No, thanks—" he peered at the name embroidered on the breast pocket of her fifties-style uniform "—Misty. I'm set."

He barely got the words out before she skittered

away, the soles of her saddle shoes squeaking on the linoleum.

As Ash watched her go, he inadvertently made eye contact with two elderly women sitting in the booth across the aisle. At his polite nod, they both clucked like a couple of startled hens and ducked their heads behind their menus, whispering.

Ash stifled a sigh. He'd have thought that, after being back in Rumor for a month or so, the stares and whispers would have dwindled, especially with the whole business of Guy Cantrell going missing and the Montana Division of Criminal Investigation linking Guy to the death of his wife, Wanda, and that gas station attendant, not to mention starting the Rumor fire. But there you were. If tongues were still wagging about Ash, it meant people's opinion of him had to be pretty bad, considering it was unswervingly Montanan to live and let live. You minded your own business and let your neighbor mind his, whatever that might be.

Except in Rumor, apparently. No town had ever been more aptly named.

He was perverse enough to have made a habit of having breakfast at the diner each morning before heading out to the Holmes Ranch, where Colby Holmes, God bless him, had hired him on immediately as a hand and had now promoted him to temporary foreman. So let 'em talk. Of course, his own close-mouthedness—about his conviction, his five years in the state pen and the reason he'd come back to Rumor at last—wasn't winning him friends. But Ash wasn't one to make explanations, not when they sounded like excuses. He'd done the crime and done the time. Period, end of story.

Shoving his plate away, no longer hungry, Ash leaned back against the banquette. Against his will and better common sense, he *had* found himself wanting to make an explanation to one person, if only to help him locate some small, minuscule positive effect in the whole disaster.

The one person he wanted to tell, though, was strictly off-limits.

Maura. Only Maura would be able to unearth the nugget of good in the past ten years of his life. *If* there was one to be found, which he greatly doubted. How could there be, when his actions had resulted in his mother dying with her son in prison and his family split apart?

Ash hid a grimace of pained remembrance behind a sip of coffee. He sure was one to talk about Maura being unrealistically trusting. At seventeen—way old enough to know better—he had believed, insanely naive as he'd been, that the "quick buck" the Brannigan brothers had bragged of making was in buying and selling cattle, of all things. And since Ash had wanted to be a cattleman since he was old enough to strap on a pair of spurs, he'd jumped on their bandwagon without even kicking the wheels.

To his credit, he'd also believed he'd be able to make enough money to support his mother and younger sister, Emmy, while his older brother was fighting in Desert Storm. Karl sent what support he could, but it wasn't enough to keep a family of three warm and fed, especially when there were medical bills to be paid. Ash gladly made the sacrifice of quitting high school after his junior year to work full-time. The problem was, the jobs a high-school dropout could get didn't pay all that well.

So he'd been ripe for the Brannigans' picking, wanting to believe that, at seventeen, he had what it took to be the man of the family.

The end of that fantasy had come swiftly, at least, when a trooper had stopped him west of Missoula driving a truck of what Ash believed was merely cattle feed, which it was. But hidden amongst the bags of feed were also a few kilos of cocaine.

He'd narrowly escaped the much-longer sentence that came with that level of drug trafficking by having the public defender appointed to him cut a deal with the court in exchange for telling what Ash knew about the Brannigans' operation. That didn't change the fact that he'd have to do some time—for that conviction as well as the other one.

Ash hunched over his coffee mug, clutched in both hands, and stared into its murky depths. There were but two paths a man could take once he found himself in a prison cell, however he got there. One was to continue down into that black hole of perdition, feed his anger with more fuel, until it sucked him and anyone he could take down with him into a bottomless pit.

It had taken a few forays down that road to give Ash a vivid picture of the future—or rather, the lack of it—waiting for him there. He'd spent a week in solitary confinement for fighting. On the cell block, there was no distinction between who started it and who was defending himself, he learned. And, bitter as he'd been at finding himself in the most unimaginable of places, he'd known his only hope for survival was to grab on to every possible lifeline.

He'd availed himself of the prison library, reading voraciously and earning his G.E.D. within the first year of his sentence. He'd quickly moved on to correspondence courses in ranch management and cattle production, soaking up knowledge as fast as he could while trying to keep his record clean and rack up points for good behavior. He'd volunteered for any and every work crew—anything to get outside those four brick walls.

It was how he'd gotten his start firefighting. When a major fire broke out, the NIFC drew from every available source of manpower, including convicts. At first Ash was only allowed to work on pickup crews, cold-trailing a fire, but his adeptness at sniffing out hot spots that other crew members missed got him promoted to the Type Two crew he'd been on the day he and Maura got caught in that firestorm.

Yes, Maura again. He still could barely contemplate how close they'd come to dying in their boots. As much as he had deemed the past ten years of his life ones he'd just as soon never have been born to live, he was glad to have been there when Maura needed him....

"Here you are, Ash," a feminine voice said beside him.

Ash glanced up and found none other than the object of his thoughts treating him to the first truly friendly smile he'd encountered inside the Rumor city limits.

The problem was, the sight of it—and her—looking

fresh and mouth-wateringly good in a pair of khaki slacks and a light-blue knit sweater that hugged her torso and made her eyes shimmer like the sun off a lake—brought back a slew of memories that Ash had just spent the past two days banishing from his mind.

And it occurred to him that perhaps he was the one who needed saving—from himself.

"Maura," Ash said curtly.

"May I join you?" Maura asked amiably.

The surprised openness in his expression instantly dissolved. "Not afraid of what breaking bread with Rumor's bad seed might do to your reputation?"

"Not in the least."

His gray eyes were their most glacial yet. "Maybe you should be."

Undeterred, Maura slid onto the seat opposite him, waving as she did to the elderly women who moments before had been casting Ash furtive glances and now frankly gaped.

"'Morning, Mrs. Alden. 'Morning, Mrs. Raymond," she said with unlimited cheerfulness. "I hope the heat and lack of rain aren't keeping you from your busy schedules this summer."

From the corner of her eye, she saw Ash bite back a smile, almost in spite of himself. The Calico Diner wouldn't be the Calico Diner without these two ladies at their usual table, nursing a cup of coffee and regurgitating yesterday's gossip.

And yesterday's news had literally been how Maura Kingsley had narrowly escaped certain death with the help of Rumor's bad seed, Ash McDonough. While she knew for a fact that this had elevated him in some people's eyes, she also knew there were others who believed that getting burnt to a crisp would have been a preferable fate.

She turned to Ash, eyeing his half-full plate speculatively. "The Fats Domino?" she asked.

He shook his head. "I favor the Chubby, the difference being I like my cured meat in strips instead of links."

"An important discrimination. And how was it this morning? I understand some people have complained in the past few weeks that none of their food here has been coming out of the kitchen like they wanted. They get the wrong order or it's not cooked right."

"Mine's been just fine," Ash answered, one long arm stretched along the back of the banquette as he slouched against it à la James Dean. "Tasty as hell. Why are you here, Maura?"

"Jilly Davis—Forsythe, I mean—told me you have breakfast here in the morning," she said, cozily setting her crossed forearms on the table in front of her as she shook her head at Misty Chambers's offer of a menu. "Frankly, with your love of nature, I'm surprised you'd frequent a place like this—all the vinyl records on the wall, the red glitter plastic-covered seats, the gold-speckled Formica tabletops, the black-and-white-checkered linoleum floor. I mean, I couldn't even begin to calculate the sheer number of petrochemicals that lost their lives in its making."

"I try not to think about it. Why are you here, Maura?" he repeated.

"I ran into the veterinarian, Valerie Fairchild, at

Jilly's flower shop. She said you'd brought Smokey in and left him with her while he gets back up to snuff. She said he appears to be in good shape, thank goodness, if still pretty traumatized. I'm heading over to visit him later this morning. Wanna come?''

His gaze didn't waver a millimeter. ''Why are you here, Maura?''

She gazed at him as steadily, willing herself not to be intimidated. He may be as cool and remote as when they'd first met, but she'd had ample acquaintance with the fire that smoldered behind those ash-gray eyes. And that fire drew her to him as powerfully as the inferno still raging less than fifty miles away.

He'd looked good in his Nomex pants and yellow fire shirt and badly needing a shave. He looked even better cleaned up and wearing what had to be his clothes for working at the Holmes Ranch: well-worn Wranglers and a chambray work shirt in pale sage green that stretched across his broad shoulders. His thick, dark hair was still wet from a morning shower and hung over his forehead in a completely captivating way.

Her attraction to him wasn't all about appearances, but it didn't hurt that he looked good enough to be his own special on the menu.

Oh, Dad was likely right that she should stay away, but she couldn't. She and this man had shared a moment that was compelling and real, as real as any she'd ever experienced before—or, she was greatly afraid, might ever know again.

As soon as she'd returned to Rumor she'd made a beeline for Jilly. Vaguely, Maura remembered that her friend knew the McDonoughs and had been friends with Emmy, Ash's sister, until she moved away. Of course, everyone knew Karl, the brother who fought in Desert Storm. He'd been one of a handful of local men who'd gone to the Middle East that the town had lauded as local heroes.

Maura could see how the contrast of Ash's mistake would have been doubly stark. Doubly disgraceful.

But she'd also learned, from Jilly, about Ash's life up until he came to disaster: how he'd quit high school to help support Emmy and their mother, gravely ill with a cancer that would eventually take her life.

When Jilly had told her that, Maura had nearly broken down in tears. How close her own family had come to losing her father to lung cancer! It had been a terrible, terrible time for the Kingsleys, and she couldn't imagine it had been any less so for Ash, especially with few resources for support.

Maura lifted her chin, determined not to be put off by his stony facade. "Jilly also told me how you maintained that you hadn't known you were carrying drugs in the truck you were driving when you were stopped."

"Don't paint me with too rosy a brush, Maura," he warned. "Did I knowingly and willingly deal drugs? No. Was I a participant in the ring that did? You bet. I deserved to go to prison, if for nothing else than being too gullible to be legal."

He was, as before, brutally honest, and she wondered if that was a result of his doing time. Her heart went out to him as she imagined the unspeakable toll prison life must have taken on that boy of barely eighteen.

Clearly, though, he was not going to be receptive to her discussing his past or her empathy for him. If only she could break through the ice surrounding his heart, she *knew* she could help him heal! Just as she could help those children and teenagers out there in the community who might be standing on just such a precipice of crisis.

The thought gave her an idea.

"Speaking of rosy views, my ranch for disadvantaged children might be closer to becoming a reality than I thought," Maura announced in an abrupt change of subject.

"Really?" Ash said mildly, but she could tell his curiosity had been piqued.

"Yes. I had a pretty significant meeting with the Rumor City Council just last night, and they're close to granting me the use of twenty acres of land south of town. It's part of a couple of sections that was willed to Rumor by a widow who didn't have any children to leave it to."

She leaned forward. "The best part is, there's already a big ranch house on the property, plus a barn and a stable, although none of them have been occupied for ten years or so."

"So you won't have to build a house to live in?" Ash asked.

"Or, just as importantly, for the kids' activities. I'll need a lot less money to get the operation up and running. I've already put in for a grant from the state that I've been told is a go if I can come up with matching local funds."

She turned her hands palms up as they rested on the

tabletop. "Now all I need to do is present my grant proposal to the Rumor Development Group to secure the rest of the financing."

Ash was silent for a good five seconds after she'd finished, and she wondered if she'd sounded as if she were bragging, especially when he saw his dream of owning a ranch as still being a ways in the future.

But that was her next bit of good news.

"That's…that's wonderful, Maura," he finally said, and she could tell from the way his eyes shone like two newly minted nickels that he meant it. "You've got to feel pretty good about making your dream happen."

His voice fell to the intimate level of before, when they were in the cave. "I can't tell you how glad I am for you."

"It's what I've always wanted," she said simply, although her heart beat with the rhythm of a marching band at the look in his eyes. And she bet they would turn to pure silver when she revealed how his own dream could come to fruition.

"And you'll never guess who's been leasing the rest of the widow's land," she said.

"Who?" he asked, his expression no longer locked up tight but open and candid as he, too, leaned forward in anticipation.

"My dad," Maura told him, breaking out into a smile. Oh, what a wonderful feeling this was! She couldn't imagine anything more satisfying than to help children—to help Ash—find the happiness they deserved.

"The thing is," she went blithely on, "he hasn't

really needed it for grazing for years...so I know he'd be happy to sublet the land to someone in the market for a pretty little spread to build his own cattle herd on.''

''Really?'' Ash said, dead quiet.

The wattage of Maura's bright smile dimmed a little as she obviously got a glimpse of his face. ''Y'know, I'm learnin' to really, *really* dislike that one word coming from you,'' she joked feebly.

This time he wasn't taking the bait. ''Stop right there.''

Out of the corner of his eye he noticed the two elderly ladies had pricked up their ears and were listening in on their conversation. ''Please tell me you half baked this plan all by your lonesome and haven't set it front of Stratton,'' he said in a low tone that he hoped didn't sound too urgent or interesting to wayward ears. *''Please.''*

''No, of course I haven't said anything to Dad.'' He was relieved that Maura took her cue from him and lowered her voice, as well, although the eagerness in it would surely rouse some curiosity. He could only pray that the two gossips on the other side of the aisle wouldn't pick up on it.

''I wanted to broach the matter with you first, since I thought you'd want to be the one to present a business plan to him,'' Maura went on matter-of-factly. ''He'll expect it to be thoroughly thought out, but I know how he thinks, so I can help with that.''

He stared at her, wondering if she was really that naive or if she actually believed he was. At his scrutiny, she dropped her gaze.

"It could work, if you truly wanted to go after it," she said with a little less certainty. "Go after *your* dream."

"You mean if I seriously wanted to forfeit any chance of getting even a fraction of Rumor to accept me back," he said. "Because swaggering into Stratton Kingsley's office and actin' like I'm entitled to a piece of prime Montana real estate that's just there for the asking, and all I lack is his blessing—well, that's sure to win *him* over. And once I do shoot, I'll be a regular Dale Carnegie with the rest of the town, winning friends and influencing people to beat the band."

Those blue eyes flashed up at him at that. "You make it sound completely impossible! You *did* save my life, Ash, and that's worth something with him even if he won't admit it."

"Of course he won't admit it. Good Lord, it's all over town that I had a hand in helpin' you out of a jam in the fire—I hear people talking about it—but has anyone said a word of thanks to me? Hell, no. They won't, either. *That's* why I think you're out of your mind, powder puff," he drawled.

The elderly ladies opposite had left off all pretense and now sat tilted toward Ash and Maura at an angle. It would have taken a hundred-pound counterweight to keep them from tipping over with their next breath.

Abruptly he leaned across the aisle, inches from their faces, and gave them his most rogue-like smile. "No need to delay your shoppin', ladies," he told them. "There's sure to be a full accounting of the go-ings-on this morning in the next edition of the *Rumor Mill.*"

Blushing, the women straightened as if pulled by a plumb line.

He shook his head in exasperation. Surely Maura was not so blinded by her optimism that she couldn't see the real situation here. He was, literally, Rumor's bad seed: he'd been planted in the same fertile Montana soil as everyone else, had received the same nurturing rain and sun as they, and yet he'd grown into the noxious weed in their garden. He was one of them and yet not, and they wanted him cut out by the roots rather than risk the chance that he'd seed more like him—or contaminate those who might come into contact with him.

Such as Maura Kingsley.

Yet he had barely been able to make himself glance away from her as she sat across the table from him. It was the first time he'd seen her with her hair loose, and it was like fire itself, the way the sunlight streaming through the window sent sparks of red and gold and bronze dancing around her shoulders. Her heart-shaped face in this light was even more heartbreakingly beautiful. Heartbreakingly innocent.

She *was* an innocent compared to him, her trust and openness day and night to his cynicism and bitterness. But he'd die to lose himself in that innocence again…lose himself in her. Yet the danger was that, instead of him being renewed by her innocence, he would taint her for life with his jadedness. He couldn't let that happen.

"Look, Maura, if getting a cattle ranch was that easy, I'd be standin' boot high in cow pies right now," Ash said ruefully. "But it's not. It's damned hard work to make it happen and to keep it going. You've only to ask your dad to know I'm telling the truth.''

"It *could* work, though, if you were willing to take the risk. Dad can be reasonable, you know." Her delicate mouth drew down at the corners in a stubborn look he recognized from their time in the cave. It also directly contradicted her words. He'd bet a week's wages that such stubbornness was a family trait, passed down from father to child.

"Even if Stratton were by some flight of insanity to find your idea a good one, I wouldn't take it," Ash said, bending toward her across the table in a continuation of his futile effort to keep their conversation private. "'Cause I wouldn't have earned the opportunity by proving my ability to take good care of the land and the animals on it.''

She leaned as insistently toward him. "Isn't that what you came back to do, though? Prove yourself? You *could* prove yourself to Dad.''

"When there's pork in the treetops, you mean.'' He had no idea why she was being so persistent, but he'd had enough. "Look, so we did share our dreams—and maybe something more—with each other in a moment of closeness, but that was all it was. A passing moment. We're back to reality now, where I'm Rumor's bad seed, and you're Stratton Kingsley's little girl.''

"But you know I'm not a little girl—or a powder puff," she said in a thoroughly intimate, thoroughly seductive tone.

Damn, it was difficult to do this when she said stuff like that and gazed at him with those soulful eyes. Her expression truly didn't contain a trace of caution or mistrust. Fleetingly he wished he knew what it was like to live in such a world, as if surrounded by an invisible force field of security, where wickedness was held at bay by a stronger power.

It drew him—*she* drew him—like a siren's call.

He had to keep trying to ignore it, for he was dangerously close to throwing away all of his own caution and mistrust.

Ash sighed. "Maura, honest to God I'm happy that you're in sight of your goal to help the kids in need around town. But you need to go find another poster boy for your cause, because I'm the wrong man for the job—"

"That's what I think, too!" came a voice from behind him, and Ash wondered for a moment if he'd spoken too vehemently to Maura and was now in line to get a tongue-lashing from a well-meaning Rumorite.

But no, it seemed the subject was the missing science teacher, Guy Cantrell.

"They say he's invisible!" said the woman Maura had called Mrs. Alden. Her face beneath her tight steel-gray perm was agog. "Invisible as the air itself!"

"Now, that don't make him a criminal, Alice," drawled a voice of reason that belonged to an older gent with a snowy white bristle-brush mustache. He obviously knew the two ladies and their habits. "I never knew Guy to've harmed a fly, even with all those chemicals he liked to mess around with out in his garage."

"Is that right?" Mrs. Raymond said with some vim. "Well then, where's Old Man Jackson? He hasn't been seen since his cabin burned down."

That got the whole diner joining in—in dead seriousness, too.

A young mother two booths down who'd been struggling to get a spoonful of oatmeal into her toddler's mouth spoke up. "Maybe Old Man Jackson's invisible, too."

"Or Guy killed him!" broke in Misty, who in her excitement dumped a Sandra Dee—otherwise known as a Denver omelet—down the front of her pink poodle skirt.

Ash supposed he ought to be glad that Guy Cantrell's disappearance and the theory that he'd started the fire had taken a starring role for the moment. He could imagine how fast his meeting with Maura Kingsley would spread if it weren't for that. Like wildfire.

"Dear heavens, what if he's peeking in our windows at us at night?" Mrs. Alden exclaimed, pressing one hand to her faded cheek. "I keep the shades pulled tight, but if he's invisible how would I know if he was standing at the foot of my bed looking down at me!"

"Honest to Pete, Alice!" the older man with the mustache said. "Guy's peculiar, but he's not a masher."

"He ain't stupid, neither," said a cowboy sitting nearby shoveling down a stack of buckwheat pancakes that was called, remarkably, the Buckwheat Special.

Ash didn't know the cowboy, but he was obviously enjoying the byplay of the townsfolk. "I mean, why in blazes would this Cantrell fella want to sneak into your bedroom when there's lots better viewin' just about anywhere else in town? What's he gonna see, anyway—how many lace ruffles ya got on your new flannel nightie?''

He guffawed, enjoying his joke enough to make up for everyone else's lack of enthusiasm. Then something happened that Ash wouldn't have believed if he hadn't seen it with his own eyes: the cowboy's Stetson flew from his head as if a hand had knocked it off. It spun through the air and hit the far wall before sliding to the floor.

The cowboy's laughter sputtered, choked and died. The diner was so quiet you could have heard grass growing.

Maybe there was something to this invisibility thing, Ash thought before mentally scoffing at such a possibility.

Finally someone coughed, breaking the tension. A patron sitting near the Stetson picked it up gingerly, as if expecting it to bite him, and returned it to the now completely subdued cowboy. He put it on his head with a shaking hand.

''Serves him right for lacking the manners to take off his headgear indoors,'' Maura whispered to Ash in a perfect imitation of Alice Alden.

Ash had to smile. ''If Guy Cantrell *is* invisible, of all things, I definitely wouldn't have a problem with insinuating myself into his good graces so I could get in on his secret,'' he said. ''I could use that kind of anonymity in this town.''

Maura giggled, and the two of them sat grinning at each other in a moment that was devoid of the worries and conflict in their lives.

A moment like the ones they'd shared in the cave.

"Do you know Michael Cantrell, Guy's fourteen-year-old nephew?" Maura asked out of the blue.

Ash shook his head. "No. Why?"

She fiddled with a sugar packet she'd plucked from the stainless steel holder. "He's a good kid, but he got into a bit of trouble with the law a few weeks back. Got caught smoking up at his uncle's house."

"Smoking's a nasty habit, to be sure, but I don't recall it being a hanging offense."

"Even if it wasn't a bad thing for him to be smoking at that age, there's the fire ban going on, and he'd apparently thrown down the still-lit cigarette he was smoking just as Sheriff Tanner pulled up. I think Max, his father, was able to keep Michael from getting slapped with a pretty serious charge by promising the sheriff Michael would do community service for his punishment. So he's working every afternoon at the community garden I run." She pointed out the window. "It's across the street in back of the library."

"A community garden?" Ash scratched his cheek in puzzlement. "What's the difference between that and a garden-variety garden?"

"It's funded partially by the city and a grant from the USDA to provide a safe place for children in Rumor to come and grow vegetables and flowers and socialize. I get a lot of kids coming every day whose parents are working."

Her blue eyes dimmed. "Some are just little ones taking care of siblings who are littler still. Others are at that age where they get bored and restless easily and need something constructive to occupy themselves."

"What do the kids do there?" Ash asked, thoroughly captivated—again.

"The younger children love to dig in the dirt and push the seeds in the ground and cover them up. The heavy work—tilling in the spring, weeding, hauling mulch and compost, and building beds—is left to the older kids, adult volunteers and the occasional person who's been given community service as part of their sentence for a nonviolent offense. There's also a horticultural component, where I do talks or interactive workshops on plant science, insect breeding, even vermiculture."

Ash had to ask. "What the hell is vermiculture?"

"Worms, my friend," she said sagely. "Worms."

He shook his head wonderingly. "How long have you been doing this?"

"This is my second year. We've only planted about ten beds, mostly vegetables, but next year I'd like to do some terracing and plant more flowers, maybe even a butterfly garden." She clasped her hands between them on the table. "The kids are into learning how to identify plants and about the environment. They even know what organic farming is," she said proudly.

He had to admire her drive and spirit. She apparently was willing, literally, to get her hands dirty when she needed to.

And to make the best of a situation while working toward a bigger goal. What was the saying? Bloom Where You're Planted. Maura had certainly done so.

"Not quite your ranch for disadvantaged kids," he murmured.

"But the next best thing," she said in confirmation

of his thoughts. "And the garden's success will help prove such a program can work on a larger scale—and that I'm the perfect person to run it."

She cocked her head to one side in that way she had. "Come by the garden after you're done working, why don't you? I get a lot of grown-ups dropping by in the evening to work in the garden and socialize, too. You might enjoy it."

To his surprise, she reached across the tabletop and took his hand in hers, squeezing it. Her touch was so electrifying, he felt it along every nerve in his body.

But he didn't—couldn't—pull away. Even if it made front-page news and had Stratton getting up a posse to hunt him down.

"Havin' me come to your garden would only cause more trouble than good for you, Maura," he said. "You know that."

"I don't know that at all, actually. Take Michael. I think it'd help him to have the benefit of your experience as someone who's amply aware of how a person can do something pretty innocently and have it escalate into a situation one can't control—and that such a mistake doesn't brand you a bad seed for the rest of your life."

He had the strongest urge to shake her. That was, if he didn't kiss the hell out of her first. She was so unrelentingly optimistic…unrelentingly naive. She had no idea what it was like to have one's options limited. She could go anywhere, do anything. The world was literally her oyster, filled with every possibility of finding that rare and elusive pearl.

He, on the other hand, couldn't even leave the tri-county area without notifying his parole officer.

Ash withdrew his hand from hers. "Maura. I'm all for you doing what you can to give these kids some constructive things to keep 'em occupied and out of trouble."

He had to give it to her straight. "But you grew up pampered and cared for and never knowing a moment of want. I find it hard to believe you could understand what I'm going through, much less what some of those kids you want to rescue are going through."

That brought the stubborn cast back to her mouth. "Maybe I can't completely understand what it's like to have suffered so. But is that any reason why I shouldn't try to understand? Or try to help?"

She stood, pulling herself to her full five-foot-and-a-hair height. And still she managed to look as regal as a lioness.

"If there is anything I don't understand—and never will—it's how you, who *does* understand, could turn away from helping them, any way you can."

And she walked away.

Waiting until the very last second before Maura Kingsley would have run into him on her way out the door of the Calico Diner, Guy Cantrell stepped aside as she walked past. She came so close to him, her sleeve touched him, which had her brushing her arm as if to shoo away the fly she mistakenly believed had lit there.

Guy had to clap his hand over his mouth to stifle his chuckle. The prank with the cowboy's hat—now *there* he'd almost lost it. He'd had to pinch himself to keep from bursting out in laughter.

The guy deserved the scare, though. He was being disrespectful to Alice and Clara who, while at times meddlesome biddies, didn't deserve to have to have some rusticated cowboy speculating about their sleeping attire in public.

Of course, Guy hadn't had any reason for switching the ladies' food orders on Misty so that she had to go back to the kitchen twice to fix them.

But frankly, he was getting bored. Guy sobered as he fell into dismal musing. He'd been in this state for over a month and he was tired of it. He'd taken to working on his formula at nighttime in the old shed that, ironically, belonged to Alice Alden. Using a flashlight Michael had gotten for him, he would pore over calculation after calculation for hours, trying to come up with another formula to reverse the effects of his ointment. Which was nearly impossible when he still hadn't figured out what it was that had caused his invisibility in the first place.

Bless Michael for risking himself to get Guy's notes on his formula for healing burns. He'd just about died to see his nephew take the fall for him. Guy could tell that the boy was worried about him, was burdened by the responsibility of keeping his uncle's invisibility secret.

Guy vowed that once he figured out how to get out of this, he'd make sure everyone knew how brave Michael had been. For now, however, he needed to concentrate on finding a cure for his cure.

Chapter Five

Maura's garden reminded Ash of a scene out of the *Wizard of Oz*.

Despite the fact that dusk was fast approaching, the activity in the garden didn't look even close to slowing. Munchkins were everywhere, squealing in their chipmunk voices as they dodged between sculptures made of wood sticks bound with twine. Morning glory vines swarmed over a tube of chicken wire that had been arched at child height over one of the gravel walkways. Huge sunflowers with seed-laden centers the size of saucers bent protectively over the two preschoolers who sat beneath them, heads together in fascination as they watched the inch-inch-inch of a caterpillar up a sunburned arm.

This was a whole lot more than only ''only ten beds.''

Towering teepees constructed of bamboo poles also dwarfed the garden's inhabitants, which did include a few adults and older children. Of course there was the prerequisite straw-stuffed scarecrow, in a calico shirt and jeans tied at the waist with rope belt, watching over the small crop of sweet corn on the edge of the vegetable patch. And beautiful, sweet, red-haired Dorothy, who passed among the youngsters bestowing the gift of a smile here, a gentle caress on a small head there.

Maura. She looked entirely in her element among the flowers, vegetables and children. Entirely able to do just as she'd vowed and save not just one soul but any who came in contact with her.

Fingers jammed into his front jeans' pockets, Ash stood on the edge of the garden, feeling like an interloper. An intruder.

Then Maura glanced up and spotted him. She broke out in a delighted smile and started toward him with that walk of hers that was incredibly sensual by virtue of its very unselfconscious wholesomeness.

Would he ever be able to even pass her on the street and not be consumed by the memory of their night together, when he'd held that goodness in his arms? How could he *not* have been utterly transformed by it, by her?

It was everything he could do not to take her again, here in this Garden of Eden where wickedness had not yet slithered in.

"Ash," she murmured when she reached him, her eyes shining. "I'm so glad you decided to come."

"I didn't think it'd hurt to check out your operation

here,'' he said gruffly, making another appraisal of the scene so she wouldn't detect the raw hunger in his gaze. ''Just point me to where I can lend a hand.''

She turned and called to one of the adults. ''Hey, DeeDee. Have you got a job for Ash?''

Ash didn't recognize the woman who left off directing the transport of a load of river rocks. She looked to be in her early fifties, with only a sprinkling of gray in the dark hair styled in one of those short, no-muss, no-fuss 'dos sometimes favored by mothers. He'd guessed that right off, given the teenage boy within sight who was the spitting image of her.

''Ash,'' Maura said when the woman had arrived at her side, ''this is DeeDee. DeeDee, Ash McDonough.''

''Pleased to meet you, DeeDee,'' Ash said, automatically extending his hand.

For some reason DeeDee hesitated, almost suspiciously, as she peered intently into his eyes.

Damn, Ash thought with an inward wince. Maybe he shouldn't have come here, practically inviting people to take potshots at him.

But before he could react outwardly, DeeDee had recovered and gratefully grasped his hand in hers. ''New to town, Ash?''

''In a way.'' He decided he may as well get it out and over with. ''I grew up in Rumor. Been away the past ten years…part of it doin' time for a drug conviction.''

Recognition sparked in her tired eyes. ''That's right. What is it everyone calls you?''

Ash stiffened at her bluntness. ''Rumor's bad seed,'' he answered, now truly wishing he'd never come, no matter how much Maura believed he had something to offer.

Then DeeDee nodded with surprising sympathy. "It's like me. I'm no longer DeeDee Reingard. I'm 'that poor, dear DeeDee Reingard.'" She concentrated unnecessarily on picking at a loose thread on her dirt-stained gardening gloves. "My husband, Dave, was sheriff here until several months ago."

Recognition ricocheted through him, followed by shock, as his mind made the connection. *Dave Reingard?*

Ash didn't realize he'd spoken the name aloud until he saw DeeDee lift her head with dignity and go on with the same bluntness. "Yes, Dave Reingard. My husband had an affair with a woman. It turned ugly. Dave killed her. He's in the state prison in Deer Lodge now. But surely you've heard all this already."

So that was what her initial suspicion had been about—not his reputation around town, but hers. And she obviously didn't know—or remember—Ash's connection to Dave.

And if DeeDee didn't know, perhaps the details of what had happened that day with Dave wouldn't have made the rounds. Of course, who was there to tell: just Mom and Emmy, who wouldn't have said a word about it on their lives.

But would Reingard, who in court hadn't had to go into detail because Ash had readily pled guilty to the assault charge, have kept what transpired in the McDonough mobile home that afternoon a secret?

Ash could hardly believe Reingard hadn't told someone. Like his wife. But it was obvious Reingard *hadn't* told DeeDee, whatever the reason.

And now Dave was in prison for a misdeed of his own.

Regardless of what she knew or didn't know, Ash couldn't help but convey his sympathy. "I'm sorry to hear about your troubles, ma'am." He hesitated, then went on, "Prison's not a place where you want anyone you ever cared for to go."

She peered at him again in that assessing way, then actually smiled, which only emphasized the two deep grooves from nose to mouth that spoke of the trial she herself had gone through.

Pointing to the strapping teenager who was helping one of the younger kids create a border with the river rock, she said proudly, "That's my youngest, Parker. It's his only night off this week, and for some reason he'd rather hang out with his mother and a bunch of neighbor kids than go to a movie with his friends."

"Where does he work?" Ash asked.

"During the summer he works days at MonMart as a bag boy, but he started morning and afternoon football practice a few weeks ago, so he's been working evenings."

She pushed her short bangs off her forehead. "I'm hoping he can go to a lighter work schedule once school starts." Her eyes clouded over. "I'd like Parker to have as full and happy a senior year as he can. He was willing to cut out football and his other activities to be able to work more and contribute to the household—he even offered to quit school, if you can believe it—but I wouldn't allow any of that."

She gazed at her son with utter and complete love. "I could never ask that sacrifice from him, even if one of us were at death's door. Especially when I've got four older than him who're happy to help out as much as possible, even though nobody's won the Montana lottery—yet, that is."

When she chuckled at her wry joke, Ash had to laugh, too, in spite of the tightness that surrounded his chest like a steel band at the similarity between the circumstances of their lives.

What sounded like a loud gasp had the two of them pivoting to scrutinize the rows of sweet corn.

"I'll go check it out," DeeDee volunteered. "Little Jerry Townsend probably came across a bug of some kind." She lowered her voice to inform Ash, "He developed a horror of them after his baby brother died of a spider bite. His mother didn't know that's what it was and that she should rush him to the doctor."

Ash watched her trot off. He had to admire her spunk. It must have been a living hell going through what she had with five kids. And now, with trying to make ends meet, having her teenage son feel he might have to sacrifice his education and future to help save the family....

Ash cleared his throat, trying to dislodge the lump that had formed there. Neither had his own mother ever expected or wanted him to quit high school to help save their family, and he realized that a good part of the reason he'd jumped into the deal with the Brannigan brothers was his desire to prove to her that his leaving school was the right choice.

And the rest, as the saying went, was history.

He felt a gentle touch on his arm and came out of his musing to find Maura looking at him with gentle eyes that seemed to comprehend his thoughts.

"And this is Michael Cantrell," she said.

A boy dressed in baggy jeans and an oversize T-shirt that proclaimed Dave Rules stood next to her. In the fading light, Ash got an impression of dark hair and glowering blue eyes beneath the backward-worn baseball cap. Although his clothes were of the style that would have hung on even the beefiest build, Michael, obviously in the throes of puberty, had not an ounce of fat on his lanky frame. It would be a few years, Ash would bet, before he'd grow into his feet, hands and features.

So this was the son of the wealthy Max Cantrell. Ash had done some discreet checking up on the boy: He was a whiz at science—brilliant, some people said—and had worshipped his uncle Guy. He'd been devastated by his uncle's disappearance and the rumors people had drummed up about him causing the deaths of two people.

Again Ash found his sympathies mightily stirred. "Glad to meet you, Michael," he said.

The boy ignored the hand held out to him, and this time Ash didn't take it personally. Clearly, this was all about teenage attitude.

"I'm only here in this stupid garden 'cause I got caught smoking out by my uncle's house," he said with an air of defiance, his glower magnifying.

"Really," Ash said calmly. "I heard about that. You must've gone over to his place because you were pretty upset about his disappearing and thought you might be able to come up with some clues on your own, since you two were so close.''

The boy blinked in surprise. ''I did want to help, even if I wasn't sure how. But Sheriff Tanner and everyone else acted like I was a…a total juvie just for tryin' one cigarette!''

Ash rubbed his chin thoughtfully. ''So you made a mistake, and you're doing what you need to make up for it. Doesn't sound like a juvenile delinquent to me— unless you keep going down that road.''

He raised his eyebrows at Michael. ''That's your choice, you know.''

The boy scowled not very convincingly. ''Yeah, I guess.''

Maura, who'd gone off momentarily to kiss a scraped knee, came up behind Michael, set a hand on his shoulder and gave it a squeeze.

''Michael's been my right-hand man since he's started helping out in the garden,'' she said, contradicting Michael's previous assertion. ''He's so knowledgeable about biology. I'm hoping to persuade him to teach the kids about photosynthesis and pollination before his time here is up.''

The boy blushed, whether with pleasure at Maura's praise or at getting caught in a fib, Ash couldn't tell. And, well, who wouldn't turn red around the ears at such approval? It was as sincere and without reserve as a baby's smile.

They were—Michael, DeeDee and himself, even little Jerry Townsend—a hodgepodge of misfits, outcasts and wounded souls, each of them with baggage of one kind or another. Yet here, in Maura's garden, was comfort and acceptance. All were equal here. All had a place.

But would all find peace? he wondered.

"I came over to ask you a favor, Michael," she went on, discreetly tilting her head to indicate a little boy nearby. "Daniel over there isn't quite grasping how the sweet peas need to be harvested without pulling the plants out by the roots. Would you mind giving him a hand?"

Michael nodded. "Sure, Maura."

She watched the teenager hurry over to the small boy tugging with all his might on a pea plant, before turning back to Ash.

"Thanks, Ash," she murmured, her blue eyes shining in a way that almost had his ears reddening, too.

"For what? All I've done is stand flatfooted in one place since I got here."

"And in that short time you've helped both Michael and DeeDee feel a little better about themselves." She cocked her head in that way she had. "You're very good with people, you know."

"People that are like me, you mean," he said ruefully, "who can't walk down Main Street without drawing stares of disapproval."

"Not at all. You simply acknowledge their mistakes—and yours—very matter-of-factly, and give them encouragement through your dignity and integrity in handling that mistake."

Warmth, like honey, poured through him. He barely managed not to duck his head and tug on his forelock, so ruffled was he by her comprehension of the exact sentiment he needed from her. He drank it in like a thirsty man coming upon an oasis in the desert.

He'd told himself all the way over to the garden tonight that he was coming to help Michael Cantrell and the other children who could use another caring, supportive adult in their lives. And that *had* been Ash's reason for coming—but he'd wanted to see Maura, as well. To glimpse again that special light in her eyes when he was the honorable, decent man she believed him to be.

Could he be that man—to her, at least, if not to his mother or sister? Maura was still untouched by tragedy—by losing faith in someone or losing faith in herself.

"Don't think I don't know what you're doing, Maura," Ash drawled, "asking me here and then bringing people over one by one so's they can get a little of the word according to Ash McDonough."

She pressed her palm to her chest and batted her eyes innocently, a Scarlett O'Hara with red hair. "Why, whatever do you mean, Ashton?" she said.

He couldn't help it. He gave in to the smile that tugged at the corners of his mouth, and she beamed back at him, again in one of those fine, rare moments.

Yeah, she sure had a way of making you feel like a new man, with all the trials of your past washed clean from your soul. He'd have to be careful not to get too used to it.

Because there was no way it could last.

Guy Cantrell ran, not caring that the gravel beneath his bare feet gouged the tender flesh of his soles. That pain was virtually nonexistent compared to the living hellfire that seemed to be consuming the rest of his body.

Fortunately, he made it behind a row of spirea bushes on the other side of the courthouse before he collapsed on the grass, writhing in agony.

It was excruciating…and terrifying. Clutching one arm by the wrist, he watched in fascinated horror as a web of veins and tendons in the shape of a hand appeared out of nothing. A hand that felt like the skin was being ripped from its very bones.

Another wave of pain jolted through him, like an electric shock, and he gritted his teeth to keep from screaming.

Blessedly, the spell passed, and he lay on the ground trying to catch his breath and let the nausea abate. As his mind cleared, he tried to concentrate on what factors might have brought the spell on in the first place, especially since they'd been coming on more frequently.

Maybe being outdoors had something to do with it. The weather was turning cooler as fall approached, and since his formula had proven to be heat-activated, perhaps conditions of sustained cold reduced its effects. In any case, with the onset of fall and then winter, he certainly wouldn't continue to have as much freedom to come and go as he'd had through the summer. Without clothing on, he'd freeze.

But he had to know what was going on with Michael. In fact, that was why Guy had been hanging about the garden, to see how his nephew was doing since getting busted outside of Guy's house. Which was not well, from what Guy could tell. Although Michael seemed to like Maura Kingsley a lot, and had even seemed to respond to that new volunteer, Ash Something-or-other. Guy truly regretted getting the boy mixed up in this, but he'd thought the only way he could return to visibility was to get his notes and go over his calculations again.

Guy sat up, propping his forearms on his knees, head down. That wasn't a problem now, apparently. He was definitely having flashes of visibility. His formula must be wearing off. Of course, he'd designed it so that once the body's natural healing mechanism took over, the substance would slowly dissolve and become absorbed into the body. He guessed that was the good news, that his hard work was a success.

He was hardly comforted.

Wearily, Guy pushed himself to his feet and headed for Alice Alden's shed and warmth and the work that would keep him up all night.

Because the bad news was, he might die before becoming fully visible again.

Kingsley family gatherings were more like command performances these days, Maura thought wryly as she rose to greet yet another brother and wife as they came into the reception room where their parents were holding court, Stratton from the comfort of one of the overstuffed, distressed leather chairs, Carolyn from the elegant Chippendale armchair that was more her style.

"Linda, Tag," Maura said warmly, giving her next-older brother's new wife a hug and getting an even bigger one from Tag. Of course, she'd had to wait until little Samantha, who'd spent the afternoon with Grandma and Grandpa, had bestowed her own enthusiastic greeting of throwing her arms around both of her parents' middles, before racing back to her occupation of amusing her new one-year-old cousin, Mei.

"How's it goin', sis?" Tag asked, giving her an extra-hard squeeze before releasing her.

"I'm doing great, Tag," Maura answered, grinning. For once he didn't ruffle her hair protectively. Tag had always been a bit of a broody hen, in the nicest way, watching out for her—and everyone else in his world. She saw in him much of her own tendency to try to play savior to every stray kitten or down-on-their-luck character who came to town.

But Maura guessed that Linda Fioretti—now Linda Kingsley—helped temper such tendencies in Tag, so that his kindheartedness was able to shine at its best.

Maura watched curiously as Tag moved almost restlessly into the room to their mother's side, then turned back to his wife.

Maura tilted her head to one side, her curiosity further piqued. "Linda…have you done something to your hair? You look different somehow. You're almost glowing."

"N-no. I got a little sun, is all," her sister-in-law said nervously, and glanced around apparently to see if anyone else had heard Maura's question.

But everyone was occupied with their own business. On Stratton's right, the oldest son, Russell, and his new wife, Susannah, who was positively radiant in her pregnancy, watched in delight as Mei tottered on chubby legs across the oriental rug toward the red ball that Samantha held out to her.

Jeff Forsythe, the cousin who was much more like a brother, perched on the arm of the sofa, his arm around the shoulders of Jilly, yet another new bride in the Kingsley family, the two of them as enchanted with the two little girls as their parents.

Of course, Maura realized, Jeff and Jilly would soon be parents, too.

Reed was the only one missing tonight, still doing his part to fight the forest fire, which showed no signs of abating. Still, Maura thought, it was good to have the rest of the family together. She could see how happy it made Mom and Dad.

Especially Dad, and especially now. He was in his element with his family, and Maura knew it always made him feel vital, as he had been feeling less and less so since handing control of the Kingsley affairs to Russell.

"Fix yourself a drink, Tag, and one for your pretty wife, then come tell me how your business is doing," Stratton said, waving his own tumbler of club soda toward the wet bar in the corner of the large room. "We've even got some of that California chardonnay that Linda favors."

"I think I'll just have what you're having, Stratton," Linda said hurriedly. She did another of those nervous glances around the room. "I…I'm a little tired tonight, is all, and I'm afraid even a sip of wine would have me snoring through dinner," she joked.

Carolyn rose and took her hand between her own, peering into Linda's face with concern. "You're not sick, are you, dear? We'd miss you terribly tonight, but perhaps it would be best for Tag to take you home. We can bring Samantha by after dinner.''

''No, no, I'm fine,'' Linda said as murmurs of agreement went up. She looked appealingly at Tag, as if asking him to rescue her, which was so unlike her that that's when Maura knew—

''Linda's pregnant!'' Tag said, the announcement bursting from him like a cork from a champagne bottle. ''That's why she's tired. But come spring, Samantha will have a little brother or sister!''

A shout of joy went up, and then it was pandemonium as hugs, congratulations and slaps on the back were exchanged among just about every one of them, expecting or not.

''That's great news, you two. Can't think of a couple who deserves this more,'' Stratton said gruffly, his remark bringing tears to Linda's and Tag's eyes as they held hands tightly.

''Oh, my dears, how wonderful,'' Carolyn said, blinking back her own rare tears. Their mother had a backbone of steel, but when it came to grandchildren, she was more akin to a bowl of mush.

Maura also knew how worried her mother had been about Samantha—and Tag, who had been through so much with Samantha's mother, Melanie.

But it seemed all was turning out right now. Maura couldn't help thinking, Don't believe in happily-ever-after, Ash McDonough? Well, I've got your happy ending right here.

The ebullient mood carried into the dining room,

through dinner and back to the reception room for dessert and coffee.

Tag, apparently realizing that the bulk of the conversation that evening had centered on babies and the expectation thereof, asked Maura around a bite of cherry pie à la mode, "So, sis, I hear you've taken young Michael Cantrell under your wing at the community garden."

Maura looked up from pouring Russell a cup of coffee from the silver service that her mother had brought with her from the East Coast when she married. Some of Carolyn's refined rituals had survived thirty-odd years in the wilds of Montana, and serving after-dinner coffee from a silver pot into heirloom bone china was one of them.

"Michael's been a great asset," Maura said, careful as she passed the full cup to her brother. Normally Carolyn did the honors, but she'd gone upstairs, insisting that Susannah remain with the adults while Carolyn changed Mei's diaper and gave her a bottle. Samantha, fascinated by her new cousin, had gone along to "help."

"Michael wasn't exactly eager to work in the garden at first, but he's been a good sport about it," Maura added.

"Thank you for taking a role in his life right now, Maura," Linda said, her eyes temporarily clouding over at the mention of her student. "He's terribly concerned about his uncle Guy."

"Dev Holmes mentioned something about Ash McDonough helping out at the garden, too," Jeff said as came back into the room with his second helping of pie. "I didn't think that sounded like Ash's kind of excitement, but what do I know?"

Maura paid undue attention to guiding a sugar cube from bowl to coffee cup. She'd been pretty careful about not mentioning Ash's name around her father since that scene in Limestone. Although she'd wanted to talk about Ash, in the worst way.

She wanted her father to know how noble and upright Ash had been in turning down her offer to introduce him to Stratton. She still hadn't given up on that idea. Not at all. She was more or less biding her time, until the two of them learned more about each other and realized that neither was the devil incarnate.

Well, now was perhaps as good a time as any to start chipping away at her father's misconceptions about Ash.

"Ash has also been a big help to me around the garden," she said casually, not lifting her head. "I don't know as I'd categorize it as excitement, but he seems to enjoy his time there."

"I didn't know McDonough had been hanging around your garden," Stratton said, disapproval evident in his voice. "Your supervisors with the Forest Service are okay with parolees volunteering with youngsters?"

That brought Maura's head up. She took a deep breath, willing herself not to react defensively. "They're fine with it, Dad," she said mildly. "He's great with the kids, Michael especially. You should see him with the teenager, really."

Stratton frowned skeptically. "More like he's there

to have *you* see him with the kid so he can get an in with you.''

"That's not true!" Maura said, her exasperation rising in spite of herself. "I *asked* Ash to come spend time in the garden because I had a hunch he could help some of those children, especially Michael. After all, Ash has had to struggle with overcoming the mistakes he's made in his life, too.''

"Michael Cantrell and Ash McDonough are nothing alike," Stratton said, jeopardizing the future happiness of his marriage by setting his coffee cup in its saucer with a dangerous clatter. "Michael's a good boy, from all accounts I've heard, who got caught smoking. McDonough is a convicted felon.''

"I've heard nothing but good things about Ash McDonough from Dev, Stratton," Jeff put in hurriedly. "Ash stepped into the foreman job out on the Holmes spread when Dev geared up his commuter service.''

He exchanged a mildly alarmed look with Jilly, who nodded.

"Ash is determined to make up for the harm he's caused the family name," she said. "I know that for a fact, Stratton.''

"And he's about as good a foreman as can be come by these days," Jeff added, throwing a surreptitious glance of apology Maura's way that told her he'd had no idea the subject was such a sore one. "Colby's been real happy with the job Ash is doing. He's even thinking of making the temporary arrangement they have a permanent one.''

Maura wanted to kiss the two of them for their

words of support, although why her own word wasn't enough for her father didn't bear examination.

But Jeff and Jilly's assurances didn't seem to matter one whit to Stratton, either. In fact, they only seemed to make him more argumentative.

"Sure, but does anyone know for sure whether he's still involved in illegal activities?" he asked bluntly. "I mean, Old Man Jackson disappeared just about the time McDonough came back to town."

"Dad!" At this, Maura wasn't just exasperated; she was horrified. "You can't be serious."

Her father shifted uncomfortably in his chair at the look his daughter sent him, but he didn't back down. "Well, part of the reason he went to prison was for assaulting an officer, did you know that?"

Maura felt as if she'd been punched in the stomach. The wind went right out of her. No, she hadn't known.

And she didn't believe it. She couldn't believe it. Her gaze shot to Jilly's. If Ash had been convicted of assault, why hadn't Jilly told her that part of the story?

"*Was* Ash in prison for…for assaulting an officer?" Maura asked her.

Her new cousin-in-law gazed back at her steadily. "It's true Ash got five years on top of the other five for assaulting an officer. But he never served any of that time, getting paroled for good behavior after his time for the drug conviction was up," Jilly said loyally. "I never learned the details of what happened. I don't know that anyone knows the full story, but I can't believe there weren't extenuating circumstances."

Which she obviously didn't want to speculate on,

either here or in private, Maura could see. She wondered what had happened, why Ash hadn't told Jilly about it.

Maura would think about that later. What mattered right now, however, was the fact that her ignorance of Ash's other conviction provided more fuel for her father's argument against him.

Which Stratton lost no time in pointing out. "You can see, can't you, Maura, why you can't be sure—why no one can be sure—what Ash McDonough is capable of? That's why I said you weren't to see that cowboy again."

Her mother's daughter, Maura set her own coffee cup down very, very carefully. She felt as if she herself were made of fine china that was close to shattering. "You did, Dad. But I am not a child. I have a mind of my own."

"That I'll readily concede," he said wryly—and not without an element of fond tolerance. "It's your judgment about men that needs maturing."

Trying to remain calm, Maura turned to Russell, the oldest of her siblings and one of the most levelheaded and fair men she knew.

"Russell, what's your take on this, honestly? Not on whether Ash is the irredeemable bad seed of Rumor or not, but on whether at twenty-two I have the right to see whomever I wish, whenever I wish or, in other words, run my own life?"

Russell looked at her with green eyes that were so like their father's. "You are old enough to make your own decisions, Maura." He paused. "You're also living under this roof, which does give both Mom and

Dad some say in your affairs—that is, aside from the fact that you're part of this family, and Kingsleys watch out for each other.''

The mild censure in his voice stung Maura. ''Do *you* think I ought to stop seeing Ash McDonough?''

''I think Dad's concerns about Ash aren't without cause, and you'd be wise to proceed with caution.''

That did it. ''Proceed with caution?'' Maura almost laughed. ''This isn't a construction zone! And I noticed that none of *you* put the brakes on your relationships. This family's had three weddings in as many months, and I've got the closetful of bridesmaid dresses to prove it!''

A strained look suffused the face of every person in the room and remained there for a good five seconds. Then they all broke out in laughter. Russell kissed Susannah on the temple, Tag clasped Linda's hand and Jeff gave Jilly a squeeze around the waist. The glances that went between each couple were intimate—and unrepentant.

Suddenly Maura felt as if she were five years old again and performing a skit with her imaginary friend Boo-Bear for the amusement of her family. She may as well face it: they would never see her as a full-grown woman with her own life to live, even if she were to earn ten college degrees or fight a hundred forest fires.

Without another word, her chin jutting and held high to conceal the fact that it was quivering perilously, Maura strode from the room.

She took refuge in her bedroom, the one place in the Kingsley home where she'd been able to express herself as an individual and not as an extension of the whole family.

The room spoke of her love of nature from every corner: the queen-size wrought iron bed was covered with an heirloom quilt with tiny sprigs of pale yellow and blue flowers and piled high with pillows in the same solid colors. On the walls were framed prints, paintings and photographs of her beloved Montana— its granite mountains, its green and gold valleys, its big blue sky.

For the first time in a while, however, Maura looked at the room with a more critical eye from the bed, where she'd flopped on her tummy. The decor had changed over the years as she'd changed and grown, but there was some memento from each stage in her life that remained: a beloved stuffed lion, a doll with red hair and china-blue eyes, an autographed photo of astronaut Sally Ride, a blue-and-white Rumor High School pennant.

Maura sighed in pure frustration. She wanted to be treated as an adult, and yet what had she done? Run to her room like a frustrated teenager pouting about not getting her way. That she had not slammed the door on her way in was small consolation.

What her family must think of her! But she *wasn't* a rebellious teenager or a spoiled daddy's girl. For years, hadn't she sidestepped allowing those protective urges in her father to take over her life *without* the usual showdowns and blow-ups of most teen years?

Still, she wasn't yet an independent woman. And everyone knew it. Russell had simply been the one to say it.

There was a knock, and with Maura's say-so, her mother entered.

"Ah, here you are," she said. "I came back down to the reception room after tending to Mei to find you gone."

Maura sat up on the mattress, dangling her legs over the edge. "I'm guessing that someone filled you in on the reason for my disappearance."

"Yes." Carolyn sighed, sitting on the edge of the mattress and clasping her hands on her thigh. "I should have known this was going to happen."

Maura couldn't help but feel a little defensive. "Known what was going to happen? That I'd still be seeing Ash, or that Dad would blow a gasket once he found out about it?"

She rose restlessly and paced to the end of the room, where she stared sightlessly out the wide window. "Mom, why is he acting this way? I mean, Dad's always been as protective of me as a cow with a runt calf, but lately he's treated me like I'm in kindergarten again!"

"That's an easy one to answer." Carolyn shrugged. "He almost lost you in that fire, dear. We both did. I don't think he's shown you one half of how much he fears for you every time you go off to work on another fire."

Maura turned, gazing at her mother in disbelief. "But Reed's the fire chief! He's out on fires *all* the time."

"Reed's not your father's 'little girl,' though," Carolyn said gently. "Your father is different with your brothers. Still concerned for his sons, but knowing that they've got to strike out and be their own men. You know that.''

She held out a hand, and Maura crossed to take it as she perched next to her mother. ''And in this instance it isn't so much about your father being protective of you generally—just with regard to Ash McDonough.'' She hesitated. ''I'll admit that I'm concerned about your association with him, too.''

Maura sighed in pure, undiluted frustration. ''Is anyone in this house remembering that I owe Ash my life?'' she asked.

''But you don't owe him your love,'' her mother reminded her, again with a gentleness that struck Maura as mother to daughter and woman to woman. ''That he's got to earn.''

Maura said nothing. *Was* she in love with Ash? If not, then she was quickly getting to that stage. He'd come to the garden to help every evening for the past week, and she'd grown used to counting on him to know just the right thing to say, the right thing to do, when dealing with some of the more difficult children. Just yesterday a seven-year-old girl who, Maura knew, was dealing with an alcoholic mother at home, had broken off at the ground all the vegetable plants in her small plot. She hadn't been able to explain to Maura why she'd done so, but Ash had sat quietly with her for a half hour, talking to her as he helped clean out the plot and plant chrysanthemums and other fall-blooming flowers. Later he had filled Maura in. The girl's mother had gotten drunk the evening before and broken her daughter's play tea set when she stumbled against its shelf on her way to her bedroom.

How could a woman *not* fall in love with such a man? Maura wondered.

Yet what was behind his conviction for assaulting an officer? Jilly had said Ash hadn't been aware that the Brannigan brothers were dealing drugs when he got involved in their operation, and Ash had confirmed that. But assaulting an officer of the law…what was the explanation for that? And why wouldn't Jilly have mentioned that part of the story and defended Ash the same way she had proclaimed his innocence in the drug bust?

Were her father and the rest of her family right? Should she stay away from the likes of Ash McDonough? If she wanted to be safe, she probably should.

But did she want to be safe, stay within the secure cocoon of her family, or did she want to spread her wings and know what it was like to fly?

"I don't want to stop seeing Ash, Mom," Maura finally said. "Who can know what's in store for the two of us? I only know I'll never have a chance of finding out if I don't take the risk."

Carolyn nodded slowly. "And Ash? How does he feel about you?"

Trust her mother to ask the one question Maura was afraid to even contemplate.

"I know he cares," she answered truthfully. But how he felt about caring for her—and her for him— was a far more doubtful matter. It was more than them being from different worlds. More than her having little experience with the kind of soul-shattering trials he'd been through. He'd hardly spoken to her of the living hell he'd endured, and she guessed that, like others who'd suffered such ordeals, he never would. And perhaps that was why both he and Jilly hadn't told her of the other part of his conviction. Only with those people such as DeeDee—or Jilly, whose home life had been so awful Ash's family had unofficially adopted her—might he feel safe to speak of his past in any detail. That, more than anything, Maura knew, was what stood in the way of their love.

Yet why was he here in Rumor, except to try to put the past behind him, to make amends and try to heal— and be happy?

And she wanted to be a part of that, however she could.

"I'm thinking...I'm thinking maybe it would be best if I moved out, got a place of my own," Maura said. "Best for me. I mean, I've scaled the highest mountain in Montana and kayaked the rapids of the Yellowstone River, but I've never fixed my own kitchen faucet or scrubbed my own bathtub."

She looked her mother in the eye. "Or had to rely upon myself and myself alone to make the kind of tough decisions I almost had to make out there in that fire."

Carolyn's blue eyes were understanding while still concerned. "You're certainly old enough to make such decisions. And you've always been able to."

She clasped her daughter around the shoulders and pressed her cheek against Maura's. "I'll miss having you around the house. So will your dad. Even though you'll be closer to home than when you were away at college, it'll be different. Then, you *were* still our little girl, just sixteen. Now, you're venturing out as a woman.''

Maura hugged her mother back. ''And I'll miss being here with you. But truthfully, Mom? I'm excited. Excited to be starting on something new.''

''Yes, you do seem to have that ability,'' Carolyn murmured ruefully. ''To take risks, set out on adventures—as you did in college, going into an area of study that's not for the faint of heart with an unflagging optimism. It's amazing.''

''You make it sound as if I shouldn't take such risks, Mom.'' Maura was thinking of Ash. ''Shouldn't I?''

Her mother pulled back enough to take her daughter's face between her hands. ''Of course you should, dear. I would never advise you not to go where your heart leads you. Your father and I worry, though, not what you'll do, but what others might do to you—and to your trusting nature.''

Maura knew her mother was thinking of Ash, too.

''I can't stop believing in the goodness and fairness of people.'' She gripped her mother's wrists, wanting at least one person she loved to understand her completely. ''I can't stop expecting the best of others, even if that leaves me open to getting hurt.''

Carolyn's mouth was trembling as she smiled. ''I'm so proud of you, dear.''

Maura hugged Carolyn again, feeling herself the luckiest person alive to have such a mother. But she was also restless and ready to take action, now that her decision had been made.

''Well!'' Maura rose. ''I guess there'll be no better time to tell Dad I'm moving out than right now.''

Carolyn looked up at her. "Actually, why don't you let me break the news to him—perhaps later tonight would be best."

She stood, smoothing the wrinkles from her linen skirt and giving her auburn hair a fluff. "I've had more experience than you in dealing with Stratton Kingsley when he's got his dander up."

Maura laughed and followed her mother out the door to return to the family gathered downstairs.

Chapter Six

Pulling the door to his apartment shut behind him, Ash headed for his pickup parked at the curb. It was Wednesday, his one day off a week. He usually reserved the day for doing errands, washing his pickup and cleaning his gear. And meeting with his parole officer, if it was the time of the month to do so.

Today, however, he intended to drive into Billings and talk to a Mr. Parnell Chapin, who was in real estate investment. A friend of Colby Holmes, he might, if the conditions were acceptable, be willing to make a loan to a convicted felon looking to put his past behind him for good.

Ash had a sheet of references and a balance statement from his savings account, which was looking pretty good lately. Steady work at the foreman level helped.

But he still held little hope that he'd make much progress today, other than learning just what might hold him back from securing the financing to lease the property Maura had mentioned.

The land her father held the current lease on.

Ever since she'd mentioned the widow's ranch, Ash hadn't been able to stop thinking about it. He'd even checked out Maura's assertion that the Kingsleys were leasing but not using a good part of it. It was true: in a market where there wasn't a whole lot of prime land for sale or lease, this parcel was perfect for a budding cattleman looking to ranch in the area.

He had to wonder why Stratton might be leasing those sections from the town if he wasn't using them. It didn't make sense. Of course, a good rancher rotated his herd and never overgrazed any part of his spread. But the word Ash had gotten was that Stratton hadn't done anything with the land since taking on the lease years ago.

Was there something wrong with it, with the soil or the grass growing on it? When he'd driven out to take a look at the sections from the road, the ranch looked to be of the same fine grazing land that these parts were known for—the kind that had made the Kingsleys rich.

So he'd keep a good attitude, a hopeful attitude, until he found reason to change it. Nothing worth having in life came easily. He'd learned that lesson in spades, hadn't he?

And he had the impetus now that he hadn't before to make his dream of a ranch happen that much more quickly: Maura. He could barely admit to hoping, even to himself, that if he went to her father as a man standing on his own two feet with a viable plan for the land, then maybe, just maybe, there might be the ghost of a chance of winning over Stratton Kingsley.

And if in doing so Stratton came around to allowing Ash to court his daughter, well…

You may not be eighteen any longer, pardner, but somehow you've still got that same gullibility that made you easy pickings for the Brannigans, he thought ruefully. Just get the damn financing. Until then, he had no business fantasizing about any kind of relationship with Maura.

Yet, just as he grasped the truck handle in his hand, he heard a familiar feminine singsong from behind him. "Excuse me, cowboy, but would you have a moment to lend me a hand?"

Ash stopped dead. Turned. "Maura?"

She stood on the sidewalk not fifty feet away, looking like a fresh-faced farm girl in a pair of bib overalls on top of a sleeveless white T-shirt and her hair held back from her face with a headband fashioned from a red bandanna. She was holding a potted plant, something fernish.

"What're you doing here?" he asked, as if she didn't have as much right to public thoroughfares as he did. She'd simply surprised him, showing up while he was thinking about her. Not that that was any kind of measure; his mind was mostly on her these days. "I mean, normally about this time of the day you're knee-deep in kids and pumpkin vines."

"I took the day off." She chucked a thumb over her left shoulder. "To move into this apartment."

Ash took a step toward her, pointing at the doorway just two down from his own. "This apartment...here?" he asked inanely.

"Yes." Her chin elevated. "I...it was time for me to get my own place. I love my dad, but I'm no longer his little girl."

His heart did a belly flop to his toes. "Don't tell me you had a run-in with Stratton over me."

"Well..."

Ash groaned. "He's gonna have a conniption *fit* when he finds out I'm two doors away. If he doesn't surround your place with an electrified fence, plus put a dozen of his top hands on guard with double-barreled shotguns, I swear I'll boil and eat my hat with a side of fries."

They looked at each other—and broke into laughter.

"I honestly didn't know that you lived in these apartments, too, Ash," Maura finally said. She nodded in the direction he'd come from. "Is that yours?"

"Yup, 2-A." He was still flabbergasted. Still... numb.

She eyed his pressed black shirt, nearly new Wranglers and spit-shined boots. "Are you on your way somewhere important?"

"You could say that," he answered, and not in the nicest manner, because he could see what was coming.

"Well, if you're not in a huge hurry, I could use some help moving my clothes and these plants inside," she said. "My brothers brought over the bigger boxes last night and helped when the furniture was delivered this morning. That is, if you've got a few minutes."

He'd have liked to be able to say he didn't have a

moment to spare, but his appointment with Chapin wasn't till later in the afternoon.

Resigned, Ash grabbed a brass pot overflowing with English ivy and a load of clothes draped over the front passenger seat of her SUV and followed her up the sidewalk. Inside, the apartment was exactly like his, only reversed. It was your basic rental, with white walls, undistinguished tan carpeting and beige countertops.

Yet in just a few short hours Maura had already transformed it into a home. In the kitchen she had propped against the backsplash a row of glazed tile trivets depicting various vegetables—artichoke, eggplant, radish, carrot, beet. A cheerful blue-and-white ceramic utensil holder bristled with spatulas, whisks and ladles. In the square, plain-as-vanilla living room, she'd placed an overstuffed, deep-wine-colored sofa across one corner, with an oriental rug in front of it at the same angle. The sofa and an armchair covered in royal blue were piled with colorful pillows in the same rich tones.

And although he carried the ivy, he couldn't imagine where she would put it. The place was filled with enough greenery to single-handedly save the ozone layer.

"That one goes here in the bedroom," she called to him from down the hall. "So do the clothes."

The bedroom?

Ash warily walked down the hallway and stepped to the threshold of the room, as if it were the edge of a cliff. It might as well have been, for all the dread it inspired in him.

For it actually wasn't the prospect of Stratton's wrath that scared the living daylights out of him. It was too much of a temptation, having her this close. Too much like his greatest dream being handed to him on a silver platter—just as the Brannigans had done ten years ago.

"Here you go," he said, holding his loads out to Maura, stiff-armed.

"Thanks." She relieved him of the hangers of clothes and gave a nod toward the far corner of the room as she hung them in the closet. "Would you mind setting the ivy on the table by the bed?" she asked over her shoulder.

Ash took three giant steps into the room, set the plant on the table, did an about-face and took three more giant steps back to the doorway, where he waited respectfully to be dismissed so he could get the hell out of there.

Finished with her task in the closet, Maura turned and regarded the plant with a critical eye. "Hmm."

She crawled across the wrought iron bed to adjust the pot an inch to the left, then sat back on her heels. "I don't know. Maybe something a little more contained, like a succulent, would work better in this spot. What do you think?"

What did he think? Actually, that maybe the entire town of Rumor was right and he was as bad a seed as they came, because what was front and center in his mind at that moment was pulling Maura down onto that antique quilt and making love to her.

"Look, Maura," he said, "I'll move anything you want, but a decorating consultant I ain't. Remember,

I've done five years in prison. If I've got a plate to eat off, a sink to wash up in and a mattress to sleep on, I count myself lucky.''

Then he headed back down the hallway to safer ground.

It took half an hour to unload her SUV, and once they had, the time was edging up on noon. Ash stood in the middle of her living room drumming his fingers on the thigh of his jeans, ready to be gone and out of reach of temptation. Or was that putting temptation out of *his* reach?

"If we're just about finished here, I had it in mind to head to Billings this afternoon," he said abruptly.

"Oh," Maura said, clearly disappointed. She didn't ask what he was going to Billings for, and Ash wasn't about to explain. "Won't you at least let me thank you by fixing you a bite to eat before you go?"

He gave a curt shake of his head. "Thanks, but no."

"But you've got to eat lunch sometime, don't you?" she persisted, leaning her elbows on the breakfast bar that separated the kitchen from the living room. The action made her V-neck T-shirt gap a little in the front. Not much, but enough that Ash could see a hint of the shadow between her breasts.

And he was back in the cave—with her lying beneath him. Instantly.

He cleared his throat. "I'll pick up a burger or something once I get to Billings."

She frowned. "Not fast food! Honest, Ash, it won't take but a minute for me to whip up something I guarantee you'll find tastier than that."

"Oh, I'll bet," he muttered.

"Pardon?"

"Nothing." He stifled a sigh. "All right."

She was true to her word and in record time put together some appetizing turkey sandwiches and pasta salad that had come from the deli at MonMart, if he had to guess. Accompanied by a glass of iced tea, it was definitely better than what he would have eaten at a hamburger joint.

They ate side by side on stools at the breakfast bar.

"I've been meaning to ask you, Ash," Maura said after a bit. "Why did you come back to Rumor?"

Ash stopped midchew at the out-of-the-blueness of her question, then swallowed with a shrug. "I told you why—to make amends and get on with my life."

"Make amends to whom, though?"

He wondered at the nature of her interest. "Family. Friends. Had my actions affected only myself, I'd have made peace with myself and moved on. Would probably never have come back to Rumor after ten years. But there're those people to think about."

"What people, though?" She seemed to concentrate unduly on a spot on the counter just beyond her plate. "Your sister, Emmy? She's in Big Timber. Your brother Karl is in Kentucky. And the people who've mattered to you in Rumor, like Jilly Davis—you've made your peace with them. So what else is keeping you here?"

He made a production of carefully repositioning the lettuce on his sandwich to buy himself some time. "It's more than just telling the people I hurt here that I'm sorry and getting their forgiveness," he finally said, wanting to be truthful without revealing the entire truth. "Although that's plenty enough reason, don't you think?"

Out of the corner of his eye he saw her turn to look at him, and knew it was with her infinitely compassionate—if not completely understanding—gaze. It had a way of disabling his defenses.

"Do you mean there's another situation you need to put right? Someone else you feel you need to make amends to?" she asked gently.

He set his jaw against that gentleness, but was only able to hold out for a few moments. "I've never been out to the cemetery to my mother's grave. She died while I was in prison."

"Do you feel you have to make amends to her?" Maura asked.

"Not so much that. I was able, before she died, to ask her to forgive me." He squinted at the black-and-white photos of Glacier Park on the far wall. "And to see it in her eyes that she did."

Ash closed his eyes, and the photos were imprinted in reverse on his eyelids. Maura's hand was warm as it covered his fisted one on the counter. "Of course she forgave you, Ash. She loved you. She'd have forgiven you before you even asked. I know it."

Opening his eyes, he took a bite from his sandwich. It tasted like sawdust on his tongue. He choked it down as best he could and pushed his plate away.

No, he didn't know what information or assurance Maura was after—maybe she wasn't after anything, and it was simply his usual defensiveness taking over again.

Or maybe it was knowing deep down that what he

desperately wanted to hide from her could not be hidden—actions of such a nature that he could barely think about them. He'd tried to warn Maura about his secrets from the very beginning, but she wasn't getting it. How could she, when she hadn't experienced anything nearly as damaging to her own spirit?

Still, Ash *wanted* to be truthful with her, as much as he could be without shocking her into turning away from him forever.

"But Emmy…Emmy hasn't forgiven me," he said. "I haven't talked to her in ten years, but I can't believe what happened doesn't still affect her life. The hell of it is, I can hardly blame her. She had to deal alone with…with everything that happened. Especially Mom's death."

Using the pretense of taking a sip of iced tea, he eased his hand out from under hers. He craved that touch from her too much for his own good. For Maura's, too.

His withdrawal didn't put her off. "How do you know she hasn't forgiven you, Ash? Maybe she has and she's just waiting to tell you that."

The warmth in her voice was the same as in her touch. Again he was compelled to close his eyes against it, and again it overpowered him, like the firestorm that had first brought them together.

"Emmy… God, she was only thirteen when I went to prison, Maura." He could hear how hoarse his voice was. "And after Mom died, she had to leave Rumor and go to a foster home in Big Timber—because neither of her big brothers were around to take care of her."

He cleared his throat unnecessarily. "You probably know that from Jilly."

"Yes."

"Yeah. What Jilly probably didn't tell you, because she didn't know, was that Emmy was placed in Big Timber because the county social worker felt that dealing with the scandal of what happened with me would have been too much for her to handle at that age."

Ash paused, wondering why, really, he felt compelled to go down this road with Maura. Maybe that was why he'd experienced such dread at the prospect of her living so close to him…of letting her closer to him. Because even if she knew the complete story, there was a chance that she still wouldn't understand. Or couldn't understand.

Or wouldn't *want* to understand.

And maybe that would be for the best—for Maura at least, if not for him.

So he went on. "When Karl got back to the States, Emmy was able to move with him to Kentucky, where he was stationed, and finish out high school."

He hesitated, setting his nerve to go on. "Five years later, she wanted nothing to do with the newly paroled big brother who'd let her down. So I left them alone—her and Karl—hoping time would kind of dull the edges of what happened."

"So how did Emmy get back to Big Timber?" Maura asked, puzzled.

"After she graduated from high school, she got her degree in nursing in Kentucky, then came back to Montana—back to Big Timber—to settle. That's what makes me believe what I did still affects her. Otherwise, why wouldn't she have moved back to Rumor, where she's got friends like Jilly?''

"I guess I still don't understand, Ash," Maura said. "If Emmy's in Big Timber, and she's the most important person you feel you need to make peace with, why wouldn't you have moved to Big Timber to do that?"

"There are people here, too, in Rumor." He heard the mounting exasperation in his voice. "I told you that."

"Yes, but you could have contacted them from Big Timber," she persisted. "Why deal with everything and everyone here in Rumor, especially when you don't have to?"

"Damn it, that's just it! I *do* have to!" Ash set the edge of one hand on the counter in emphasis. "Don't you see? Emmy came back to Big Timber, not Rumor. And it wasn't because she had a rip-roaring love of the town she'd only lived in a year. It was because she didn't have the choice of coming back to Rumor where she *does* have ties. That's why I came back here. I won't have the whole town of Rumor forever thinkin' I'm a bad seed! I made a mistake, and I paid for it. Dearly. But Emmy, our friends…I won't have one person feel ashamed to have known me, or to feel he or she has to defend me to others."

He faced her squarely. "Admit it, Maura, that's what you're having to do, isn't it? I don't need to hear it from you directly that the reason you're here in this apartment is because of me—because of defending me."

"Yes." Her voice was very soft.

"I *knew* it."

Ash rose, needing to move. He took a few aimless steps into the living room. "Lord knows I don't want that for you, Maura. I'd rather go to prison again."

He shouldn't have gotten into this with her, because there really was no chance that she'd understand—or that her understanding would change the situation between them. The only person who could, the only person he'd ever talked to about Emmy or about returning to Rumor was Karl.

His older brother made a point of calling Ash from Kentucky once a week. They didn't always talk about Emmy, though. Ash often asked Karl for his advice— about leasing land for his own ranch. *About Maura.*

Karl told him to hang in there, that he'd get the land based on his own hard work and merit, that things would get better all around if he just kept at it. That Emmy would forgive him. That Rumor would.

About what would happen with Maura, Karl couldn't say.

"Ash," she said from behind him. "You'll talk pretty readily about what happened with the Brannigans and the drug bust. But you haven't said a word about the other charge you were convicted of—assaulting an officer."

Ash felt his whole body turn to stone. "What about it?"

"What happened there, Ash? It's got something to do with Emmy, doesn't it?"

He crammed his hands into the front pockets of his jeans. "DeeDee told you, didn't she?" he said dully.

"DeeDee? Why would she tell me anything?"

His shoulders eased a bit. Could it really be that the details of what happened that afternoon had never become grist for the rumor mill? It seemed a miracle that they might not have.

"Well, I can't believe it's been kept a secret for ten years," he said, buying time, fishing for information. "You could probably ask anyone in town."

"I don't want to hear it from anyone in town. I want to hear it from you. Believe me, Ash—nothing you could tell me would make me feel differently about you."

He turned to face her and searched her gaze for a long moment. Then he shook his head.

"No," he said. He simply couldn't tell her. For all his talk of being honest with himself and others about his past, he wasn't about to explore this subject with Maura, the one person he should be completely honest with.

And that was the real hell of it.

"Why won't you tell me?" She spread her hands on the counter in front of her. "I know I don't know you very well, Ash, but what I do know is that you're not the sort of person who assaults people for no reason!"

"That's just it. You *can't* know anything of the like, either about me or what I've been through."

He gritted his teeth, still at war with himself. With her, for he saw in her eyes that ever-present desire to understand.

"I've done hard time in prison, Maura," he said, his voice hard and hollow, like the sound of walking on drought-ridden earth. "The loneliness is crushing. It takes every bit of your will not to succumb to it. And all the time you're getting more and more weary, like you're trying to swim upward through a waterfall…''

So sometimes you do. You do succumb to it. And in doing so you come face-to-face with every failing, frailty, weakness and vice within your soul.''

''It must have been awful for you, just awful,'' she said, her voice cracking. She didn't turn away.

''Awful?'' He gave a mirthless laugh at the incredible inadequacy of the word. ''It was a living hell. That's what I'm trying to tell you, that it changes a man forever. You can't go back to how you were before, you can't bring back feelings, like hope, just because you want to.''

He shook his head slowly. ''And you can't make people understand how you can feel that way, no matter how much you may want them to or how much they want to.''

Her already fair skin paled even more. ''Are you trying to tell me something, Ash, about us?''

''Yes. I'm saying that, while I'm as committed as ever to making peace with who I've got to, to moving past the mistakes I made, to one day owning my own spread, don't mistake that for hope, Maura.'' He was as blunt as he'd ever been. ''Not the kind of hope you have or want me to have, just on your say-so. I'd be fooling you—fooling myself—to believe I could ever share with a woman a real hopefulness for the future.''

If her face was pale before, now it turned translucent in its lack of color. She was still as death, in fact, and Ash experienced both relief and deep disappointment.

Relief that he had finally convinced her. Abysmal disappointment that she could be convinced.

With a strange sort of detachment, he glanced at the clock above the sink. He still had plenty of time before his appointment with Chapin, but part of him wondered what was the point? This conversation with Maura had certainly given him the double shot of reality that he'd obviously needed—dreaming of going to Maura's father with a proposal for that land, thinking it would turn around the rancher's opinion of him, hoping Stratton would then miraculously give Ash his daughter's hand.

He must have been insane to even entertain such thoughts.

"I gotta go," Ash said.

His move toward the door jolted her out of her trance, however, and Maura grabbed his hand as he turned.

"No!" she cried. "I won't let you just say that and leave!"

"You can't much stop me," he said, trying to extract himself from her grip.

She held on for dear life. A bulldog had less tenacity. "You don't think I'm struggling with believing in us, that I haven't had my doubts? I've got practically my whole family questioning the wisdom of what I'm doing, getting an apartment, caring for you!"

"They're not wrong to be afraid for you, y'know."

"Maybe not." She stared up at him with those blue eyes that would always be his undoing. "But it's not for them to say, just like it's not for Rumor to say. It's between you and me. And while I know we've got some things to work out that to you don't seem possible, opting out because of my family's or the rest of Rumor's opinion of you isn't right!''

Her hand was so small in his. For someone of her size and gender, she had the courage of Sitting Bull. Yet he hadn't been entirely off the mark when he'd dubbed her a powder puff: bunny soft and about as substantial as a feather. He had an overwhelming desire to take her into his arms, to hold her safe from anyone or anything ever hurting her.

The problem was, *he* was the someone she needed protecting from.

''Maura.'' The word was as much of a warning as he could make it, with her touching him.

She wasn't deterred. In fact, she took the final step between them and wrapped her arms around his waist as she laid her cheek against his chest. He bit the inside of his cheek to keep from groaning at how good it felt. How good she felt.

She was not turning away from him.

''You aren't a bad seed, Ash,'' she whispered. ''You're a very, very good seed. I saw that from the first.''

She turned her face up to him, her eyes as blue as a glacial lake. ''I'd plant you in my garden.''

And he would soak up her attention and understanding as if they were sun and rain, Ash thought. His gaze had a will of its own, dropping to that luscious pink mouth of hers. Yes, he would soak her up, take her into himself, become one with her in that endless circle of life.

Unable to resist the pull of her and that continuity, he bent his head to kiss her.

Her lips were petal soft and full, Ash thought as she leaned toward him and he wrapped her in his embrace. Kissing her was like kissing the sky. Holding her again was like holding heaven in his arms.

She felt so good. So damn good.

"God, Maura, what you do to me," he muttered against her lips. "I want you so much, holding back from taking you right now is like trying not to breathe."

"Then don't hold back," she murmured, her splayed fingers curling against his chest. "Make love to me, Ash. Please. Let yourself love me. Please."

He shook his head, and the action only aroused him more as his mouth brushed against hers. He fought for sanity. "I can't risk it, Maura. There's too much at stake here."

She reached up to bury her fingers in his hair and tug his head up enough so that they could look into each other's eyes.

"I know you're afraid, Ash," she said. "You've lost so much already. And there's so much you feel you've got left to do. Learning to deal with the disappointments in your life—in yourself—so you can move on."

Lovingly she brushed back his hair from his forehead. "And that'll come, Ash, I know it will, as long as you keep at it. But never risking yourself again isn't the way to go. It's putting yourself out there that'll help you resolve these feelings."

"How can you know that, though?" he asked almost desperately. "How can you know for sure?"

She frowned momentarily in thought. "Think about how it is fighting a fire. It's terrifying, it's so big and ferocious. How could one person's efforts make a difference? But you put yourself out there anyway, despite your terror. You fight it however you can. You save whatever and whomever you can. And you do make a difference."

Now she smiled, oh, so tenderly. "And I, for one, will be forever grateful that you made *that* effort and took *that* risk. Because you saved me."

His hands clenched around her waist, holding her away from him, a final bid to find tenuous control. "God, Maura, you make it sound so clear-cut. So…easy. And it just isn't. That's where we're different. You *haven't* experienced the kind of disappointments I have. You haven't been disappointed in yourself."

"Maybe not to the extent you feel you have, Ash." She reached up and took his face between her hands. "But I do know real fear, you know. I'm afraid right now, in fact," she whispered. "Afraid *not* to risk myself, and never know the happiness I deserve."

And when she drew his head down so that her mouth again fused with his, Ash knew he should be stronger, should have more control, should do what was best for her.

But he could barely think, she filled his senses so. With a low growl, he clasped his hands on her waist and lifted her so that he could kiss her more deeply. She wrenched another growl of pleasure from him when she wrapped her arms around his neck—and her legs around his waist.

He slid his hands down to her bottom, caressing her. She was so petite, so perfect. And even if it damned him to admit it, Ash knew it would have taken a far, far better man than he to resist this woman.

Yes, here he knew that whatever fears held him back he must overcome and not let her down.

Without breaking their kiss, he lifted her more securely against him—she was light as air—and carried her down the hall to that virginal-looking bed. He bent, with her arms linked around his neck, and pulled back the quilt he knew without asking had been passed down from some Kingsley ancestor.

Slowly he placed her against the pillows and after yanking off his boots, settled himself along the length of her.

He let himself explore her as he hadn't had the luxury to do before, taking his hand on a stroll along the fine line of her collarbone, down her arm to her tiny wrist to her fingers, which he engulfed in his.

"You're so delicate and fine—like expensive china," he muttered. "I'm afraid I'll hurt you."

"I'm not china, though. I won't break."

She watched him through half-closed eyes as he continued his fascinated exploration. "Do that thing where you brush my hair from my face with the back of your fingers," she whispered. "I loved that when you did it before, it was so tender."

He obliged and was rewarded with a soft sigh as her eyes drifted shut. Oh, yes, he would love her with all his might. This time they didn't have the distractions of the cold cave, its rock-hard floor, its dank smell to contend with. Still, Ash had a feeling that the two of them could have been standing in the middle of a blue norther and it wouldn't have detracted from the moment.

"You're so beautiful," he said, his thoughts reminding him. "Even when you had soot a half-inch thick on your face and were wearing that awful, unattractive fire gear and steel-toed boots, you looked good enough to eat with a spoon."

Maura laughed, and it was so satisfying a sound he was compelled to make her laugh again.

"Of course, *anything* would have been tastier than that MRE you opened up and spread out like it was Thanksgiving dinner," he drawled. "In fact, I think you *like* how those things taste."

She punched him playfully in the chest. "I do not!"

"Well, now that you're on your own, you better start liking 'em. I've got a feeling you probably never had to do anything to make a meal happen, except put your order in with the chef."

"We do *not* have a chef!" Maura protested through her giggles. "And I know enough about cooking not to starve."

Ash deftly caught her arm by the wrist at the next salvo. "You know the number to the deli department at MonMart by heart, is what you know."

"And I suppose you're a regular Chef Boyardee in your own kitchen."

"By that I'm sure you're implying I eat my dinner out of a can." He lifted one shoulder. "I won't kid you. I'm prone to all the habits of bachelorhood, including eating over the sink each night using the same fork. And just so you know, I prefer canned beef stew over SpaghettiOs. In fact—'' he held up a hand, fingers crossed ''—me and Dinty Moore are just like this.''

His tactic worked: Maura broke into laughter that sounded like bells ringing on a Sunday morning. Her face was lit from within with happiness. That he had a hand in making her so was the greatest feeling a man could have.

No, he couldn't resist her. Didn't want to.

Ash kissed her smiling mouth, and she arched against his hand as he caressed her softness from hip to breast. He undressed her as slowly and as sensually, delaying removing his own clothes so that he could concentrate on her pleasure. And once he had, he wanted to see her, touch her, taste her in every way possible.

He did all of those things, thumbs bumping over her taut nipples, making her moan. His tongue trailing downward from rib cage to abdomen and beyond. And he watched how each action made her gasp or moisten her lips or arch against him.

Ash sat up, tugging his shirt out of his jeans and unbuttoning it with the other hand. If he didn't make love to her in the next few minutes, he'd die.

Then he was lying naked beside her, making him wonder how he could ever have even considered forgoing this feeling again.

Still, he needed to be honest with her. ''Maura, I've got to tell you now, before we go any further...I've still got misgivings about us. I don't want to lead you to believe different.''

Ash looked at her solemnly. "Just wanting to save someone doesn't mean you'll do it." He meant himself—and her wanting to be that savior of his soul.

"I know." She edged her calf up the outside of his, her knee pressed to his thigh, so that they touched intimately.

Ash fought for a coherent thought even as he reached down to grasp her behind the knee and tug her more closely against him. So close. "There's a lot going on besides this…this connection between us that's got an effect on things."

She shifted her hips, and both of them gasped as they became one.

"But as long as we do have *this*—this connection— those other matters can be worked out," she murmured.

"Can they?" he asked raggedly, and he was again surprised at the desperation in his voice. Desperate for her to believe, even if his own faith in the future—in life—still lay in ashes.

Her eyes were cloudy with passion. And conviction. "Of course they can. I don't know how, Ash. I just know they can."

Neither did he. Yet he made love to her, slowly, sweetly, passionately, so that when she cried out beneath him, it was all he needed to glimpse the promise she so believed in.

And for that one moment, he too believed.

Maura opened one eye and peeked at the clock on the bedside table. One-thirty. She didn't dare move— didn't want to move. In fact, she could have stayed forever just as she was at that moment…safe in the warm embrace of Ash McDonough.

An apparently dozing Ash, she guessed, judging from the pattern of his breathing, the occasional twitch of a muscle in the arm around her. She quelled the urge to move her hand across his chest and down that arm, to soothe any restlessness in his sleep or soul, however she could.

But it wouldn't be as simple as that. She'd known it even before today's conversation with him. He was still so tormented by how he'd hurt the people he cared for. Maura wanted nothing more than for Ash to find relief from that burden. No, she couldn't know what he'd endured, couldn't take that burden away from him, but she could do something to help: she could love him and believe in him.

It had to be enough.

"Mmm," Ash murmured drowsily, stirring. "What time is it?"

"Half past one or thereabouts," Maura answered, giving in, now that he was awake, to her impulse and massaging his chest with her fingers.

He gave another "Mmm," this one of pleasure, and tucked her closer to his side, her head on his shoulder. "I would gladly give a couple months' pay to be able to stay here and let you have your way with me again, but I've got to get goin'. I've got some…some business I need to attend to in Billings."

"Actually, I've got some work to do on my presentation," Maura admitted.

"What presentation?" he asked, his breath ruffling her hair.

"To the Rumor Development Group. They're meeting tomorrow night, and I'm on the agenda to make a formal presentation on my plans for the children's ranch." Idly she swirled a finger in his chest hair. "I've already drawn up a budget and made a schedule for the modifications and improvements and how much they'll cost. I want to do an actual site plan that shows how the improvements will be made. The poster board is bought. I just need to draw the site plan on it."

"Sounds like a pretty thorough job for something that I'd understood was pretty much in the bag," Ash observed.

She stretched, then settled back against him. "I think it is a go, for all intents and purposes, unless any red flags come up. But I want to show the group I've got all my ducks in a row, not just for my sake but for Dad's, too. He's a member of the development group, and I want the rest of the people to feel that even if I wasn't Stratton Kingsley's daughter, this would be a good project to fund."

"Mmm," he said once again, and this time Maura heard something in his tone that could only be called skepticism.

"What?" she asked.

Her head rose as he shrugged the shoulder her cheek rested on. "Do you think it'd work as well the other way around…say, with someone who wasn't connected coming in with a sound proposal?"

"I don't know," Maura answered frankly. She propped herself up on her elbow so she could look at him. Something in his tone made her think this might be more than idle conversation. "What kind of proposal?"

His gray eyes were half-closed, the expression in them veiled. "Oh, maybe using other parts of the widow's spread in a way that still preserved it."

It struck Maura what he might be tip-toeing around about—his own plans for a ranch.

"Well, I don't think the city council or the development group would turn down a sound plan out-of-hand." She answered, carefully nonchalant. "I know for sure my dad wouldn't, at least. He is a fair man, despite how he's been toward you."

She looked at him. "Why do you ask, Ash?" She wanted him to open up to her as he had in the cave.

But if his expression had been unreadable before, now it was completely closed.

"I'm not as gullible as I was ten years ago, Maura," he said neutrally. "There's a difference between being a fair businessman and protecting your…interests."

She had to admit it hurt just a little that, even after the closeness they'd just shared, he still felt he needed to be wary with her. Of her. Because she was Stratton Kingsley's daughter.

She wanted to urge Ash to give her father a chance. To give himself a chance to let her father know him. She knew that if Stratton had the opportunity to become acquainted with Ash that his attitude would change. She *knew* it. Neither of them would ever believe it, but they were a lot alike.

"It does continue to puzzle me, though," he said abruptly.

"What does?"

"That in spite of how your dad's been with me, he *does* strike me as someone who wouldn't have gotten where he is without a keen sense of justice—and decency."

He trailed a fingertip down her cheek. "And I know he wouldn't have been able to produce a daughter with those qualities without having 'em himself."

She was so surprised by his comment she barely felt his kiss as he let her go, swinging his legs to the floor and sitting on the edge of the bed before she could react.

"Now, where do you suppose my underwear got to?" he asked.

Suddenly inspired, Maura pointed upward. "Is that them swinging around on the blade of the ceiling fan?" she asked innocently.

Ash glanced up—then glared at her as she smiled at him. "You keep saying how gullible you were," she said, "but I got news for you, cowboy. You still *are.* And it's not a bad thing."

He peered at her intently. Then, after a long moment he smiled back and, although it didn't reach to the very back of his eyes, Maura could tell he was making the effort to trust.

"*Really,*" he drawled, the dangerous glint in his silver-gray eyes sending a thrill through her as he turned and leaned back over her, arms propped on either side of her as his eyes made a thorough perusal of her naked torso. "Just so you know—that's the last time I'm letting you take advantage of me."

Maura snaked her arms around his neck, pulling him close once again.

''I hope it's not the last time you take advantage of me,'' she whispered. *''Really.''*

Chapter Seven

"Hello, Emmy?"

There were ten beats of silence on the other end of the line, seconds in which Ash nearly dropped the receiver despite the death grip he had on it.

"Ash," his sister finally said. She did not sound surprised. Or happy. "I'd heard you'd come back to Rumor."

"A couple of months ago. I've been working for Colby Holmes on the family's spread as temporary foreman."

"Jilly told me."

He wondered if Jilly had also urged Emmy to reconcile with him, as she'd been urging him to do on a regular basis for more than a few weeks. "I'm hoping Colby'll make it permanent."

He wouldn't have dreamed of telling his sister about

his hopes for having his own spread. Hopes that were somehow in sight of becoming a reality.

That was right—by some miracle, Parnell Chapin had decided that backing Ash's foray into ranching was a good bet.

Colby's recommendation had helped enormously. Ash owed his boss big-time. Yet having a spotless record since being released from prison, including never missing one meeting with his parole officer, which Larry had been more than willing to avow to, had helped, too. Ash would actually miss Larry, because Ash's move to Rumor had put him out of Larry's purview. It was a good thing Ash had gotten his parole officer to speak for him before Ash was reassigned; it would have been much more difficult to secure Chapin's financing if he hadn't.

Even so, he hadn't been given as much capital as he'd asked for, but used conservatively, and supplemented by his savings, he hoped it would be enough to make it worth Stratton Kingsley's while to sublet a portion of that land and for Ash to buy enough cattle to get a decent herd going. He'd have to live in town till he could build a house, but hopefully he'd be able to lease one of the outbuildings on the property where Maura would be setting up her children's ranch.

And, Lord willing, and the creek didn't rise, ranching such land would provide him with a decent living. With a decent life, for himself at least.

He couldn't permit himself to think of putting Maura into the equation. Not after making love to her the other afternoon. It had made the possibility so tangible he could almost taste it. He had to guard against the tide of emotion sweeping him along or he might do something rash.

"Even if working at the Holmes Ranch isn't where I eventually end up," he told Emmy cryptically, "my intent is to stay. For better or worse, this is my home."

"I see."

His sister sounded so…indifferent, as if where he was and what he did didn't matter. But then, wouldn't she also have had to make a living of trying not to care too much?

It must be a McDonough trait. The family likely had the patent on it, in fact.

The silence rose up between them again. He was at a loss as to how to go on, how to break the ice that had had nearly ten years of winter to become thick as a house and hard as brick.

But he had to try. This was his only sister. If she told him to go to hell, well then, at least it'd be out there. And at least he knew the route, having been there and back.

That he was willing to go there was obviously due to Maura Kingsley. Knowing she'd been willing to risk her father's ire meant a lot. Her belief that things would work out, somehow, some way, was starting to rub off on him. Otherwise he wouldn't have contacted Emmy so soon.

"Look. Emmy." He swiped the beads of perspiration from his lips with the edge of his index finger. "I know I haven't been the best brother to you, and I probably don't have a right to barge back into your life. That's part of the reason why I haven't called before now. I guess…I guess I wanted to be back in

Rumor for a while, establish myself…see if I could sort of win over a few people here so you could see that I was in earnest. So you wouldn't have to feel ashamed to come back yourself…''

Ash bent his head, kneading his forehead. Damn, this was hard, especially when there was nothing but silence on the other end. He'd rather have gone back to prison—

No, he never wanted to go back there again, no matter what he faced here on the outside. He hadn't succumbed to despair then, and he wouldn't now. He still hadn't gotten a firm grasp on how to make a life for himself on the outside, but he wasn't ready to pack it in just yet.

"Emmy, I don't think I've ever really said I was sorry for what happened," Ash said on a rush. "For what I did, I mean. I made explanations up and down about how I didn't know there was cocaine in that truck. But I never said I was sorry. For letting you down. For letting Mom down, right when you both needed me the most…you know, that day when the deputy came…''

Ash hunched forward in his chair, elbow on one knee as he rubbed his forehead. He couldn't say it.

Apparently, though, Emmy had no such problem. "For breaking Dave Reingard's nose when he came to take you into custody for missing the hearing for your trial, so that Mom and I had to watch while you got wrestled to the floor and then got hauled off in handcuffs sportin' a bloody lip and a black eye.''

Ash's laugh held not a bit of mirth. "You've always had a knack for calling it like it is, Em.''

"You made Mom beg for you, Ash. Her worry for you made her sicker than she already was."

He swallowed, hard. "I know that was wrong, what I did that day. Intentionally wrong, which the drug bust wasn't. And I may've done the time for the drug crime, but I'll be paying for the rest of my life for the pain that confrontation caused you and Mom. Em...I haven't been to visit her grave, Em," he rasped, his throat so tight he could barely draw a breath.

This time the silence dragged on for minutes.

"All I've got to offer you is an apology," Ash finally went on. "I'm sorry. I'm asking for your forgiveness, and I hope you'll find a way to give it, maybe not now, but someday."

He stopped talking. He had nothing else to say. Even if he had, he didn't think he'd have had the energy to form the words, for suddenly he was dog tired. Weary to his bones.

He shouldn't have hoped.

Then a tentative "Ash?" sounded in his ear.

"Yeah?" His heart thudded.

"I...I'm working the night shift right now at the hospital, so I don't have many evenings free. Tuesday's my day off, though." There was an instant's hesitation, then she went on, "I could fix supper."

A baptism of relief washed over him. There was so much yet unsettled, he knew, but this was a start. And he knew his sister wanted to make that start. It was like his own personal miracle.

"I...I'd like that, Em," Ash said roughly. "A lot."

Remarkably—blessedly—she gave a laugh that he hadn't even known he'd missed. It made his eyes sting.

"You'll be relieved to know I learned how to cook, so there's no fear I'll give you the heaves like I did with the half-raw chicken I fried that one time."

His own laughter bubbled upward from his chest. "Hell, Emmy, you were only twelve, and doin' the best you could."

"And you were only seventeen, Ash," she said gently, offering yet another gift, "and doing the best you could."

At the knock on her front door, Maura virtually flew to it, whipping it open lest the person on the other side give another knock.

Because she knew who was calling on her: Ash.

She gave him a smile of relief and anxiousness that she could see piqued the hypersensitive awareness he'd no doubt developed in prison.

"Ash!" she said brightly, tiptoeing to press a quick kiss to his mouth, hoping to distract him. "Did you get my note?"

He lifted one eyebrow. He held the scrap of paper in his hand. "You wanted me to stop by after I got off from the ranch?"

"Yes." She realized she kept him standing on the stoop like an unwelcome door-to-door salesman. "Yes! Come in, please."

As he stepped past her, she did notice he was still in his work clothes and gave an inward groan at her tactical error. Not that there was anything wrong with the sight of Ash in a pair of dusty Wranglers, scuffed boots and perspiration-stained chambray shirt—at least not to her eyes—but she wished she'd asked him to come over after he'd showered and changed. It might make a little bit of a difference, that was all.

And she knew they both would need all the help they could get.

Well, there was nothing to be done about the fact now except make the best of it.

"Would you like something to drink?" she offered. "Beer? Wine?"

"A beer would be good." Now that she had a moment, she noticed a certain air of electricity about him. It virtually radiated from him.

"What is it, Ash?" she asked.

He gazed down at her with a strange mixture of hesitation and eagerness. "I...I think I may have some good news coming my way."

"Really! Ash, what is it?"

His gray eyes had turned positively silver. They shone with some inner light. "Now, I don't want to speak too soon and jinx myself, but..."

His voice trailed off as something behind her caught his attention, and Maura turned to see the appetizers she'd set out on the breakfast bar. And the tumbler of club soda and ice that had already been poured and sat on a coaster on the end table next to her own glass of wine.

"Are you expecting someone else?" he asked with some measure of suspicion.

She wanted to hear whatever it was that put that unique look of hope in his eyes, but she knew she'd best come clean with him right now while they had a moment alone. What could she say, though, that wouldn't have him heading straight out the door again and completely spoiling this moment?

And Maura didn't want him to leave her apartment right now. She knew if she could just get both men through the next half hour, they'd see eye to eye. Then Ash's good news would be the cherry on top.

"No, there's no one else coming but you," she belatedly answered his question. "You, that is, and—"

"You're just like your mother," boomed a voice from down the hall. "I've never seen the like of two women for crowding potpourri and scented candles in one bathroom. Stinks the whole place up to be damned—"

Ash had stiffened at the first sound of the voice, Maura noticed with a sinking heart. Now, as her father came around the corner and the two men encountered each other, it was as if they'd both experienced a jolt of electricity.

Stratton's florid complexion turned even redder. Gray eyebrows lowered over hard green eyes. Ash's own eyes turned to steel. The two men eyed each other with the distrust of their first meeting, as if primed for the other to make the slightest twitch so he could draw his gun and come back shooting.

"What's he doing here?" her father asked her curtly, as if Ash weren't standing right there.

Maura tried not to be discouraged. *Someone* here needed to keep a positive attitude. "I invited him. And I didn't tell you because I knew you wouldn't come, Dad. Just like I knew if I'd told Ash you would be here, *he* wouldn't have come."

She wrinkled her nose. "Honestly, do you think I wouldn't have figured that out at least?"

They continued to stand squared-off in front of each other. "Won't you both just sit down and stay for a while? For me?" she asked.

There was a long silence, then her father grumbled something that sounded like "Damned if I'm leavin' you alone with this cowboy" as he took a seat beside the tumbler of club soda.

Ash's shoulders eased visibly. "I'll have that beer now, Maura," he said calmly, and she breathed a sigh of relief. So neither of them was going to leave. At least not yet.

She got Ash a cold one from the refrigerator before easing onto the opposite end from her father on the overstuffed sofa. Ash, still with that caution of a gunslinger at a poker table, sat near her in the armchair across from the sofa, his gaze never leaving her father.

Tension radiated from them both, making the entire room feel like the inside of a pressure cooker.

Suddenly, her brainstorm to put the two men together didn't seem so brilliant. She'd been riding high on the emotional and physical connection she'd found with Ash, certain that with her love and support he would be willing to take a few more risks, to believe that on the other side of those risks could be the very thing he wanted most in this world.

But he still had a long way to go to owning that outlook. Oh, she knew that—knew that it would take hard work and facing the demons inside, for she also knew that there was still more to the story involving his assault conviction that obviously still had a very powerful effect on Ash.

"I suppose you're all wondering why I called you here," she joked feebly. She cleared her throat. "Actually, I thought it would be nice if you could get to know each other better."

She was betting on both men not being outwardly antagonistic, for her sake if nothing else. She was glad to see she was right—so far.

There was another extended, awkward silence, and then Stratton said gruffly, "I hear Colby has got a pretty good fall crop."

"Every hand on the Holmes Ranch has worked his tail off to raise a decent bunch of cows to take to market," Ash answered civilly—and much too modestly to Maura's thinking.

"I heard Dev Holmes say that the ranch would never have done so well this season if he'd still been in charge, instead of Ash," she chimed in.

Stratton actually gave a short nod. "Neither Colby or Dev's one to overpraise any more than he'd stint on it when it's due."

Ash blinked in obvious surprise at the roundabout compliment. "The drought and fires haven't done us any favors, that's for sure," he said.

Her father snorted his agreement. "If we don't get some precipitation this winter and next spring, I don't know what cattlemen in these parts are gonna do."

Maura congratulated herself on how well this was going. Then Ash sat forward, forearms on his knees and beer bottle clasped in both hands before him, in seeming innocuous interest. There was something in the action, however, that struck her as calculated.

"You've ranched here all your life, though. You've gotta have some sections you've held off grazing in case of just this kind of emergency," he observed.

"That and quite a few acres planted in grain that'll supplement winter feed," Stratton agreed. "A rancher'd be a fool to overuse any part of his land, even in good times."

Maura couldn't have asked for a better opening.

"I've been wondering. There's that land you're leasing from the town, Dad. Have you got specific plans for it?"

Out of the corner of her eye Maura noticed Ash's expression turn momentarily blank, then close up tight. It must have to do with her first idea, that time in the diner, to go to her dad about Ash subleasing that land.

Things had changed since then, however. Ash was known to more people around town—DeeDee and the other adults who came to the garden, her son Parker and Michael Cantrell, Colby and Dev Holmes—as being a hard worker, an understanding mentor and a first-rate rancher.

Please, she silently prayed, let both Ash and Dad be open to the idea.

"Not at the moment," Stratton answered her question. "I mostly took the lease so's to help out the town. The money goes to the development group to fund projects and make recommendations to the city on such things."

"And you're a member of the group," Maura reminded him. "So you've got a lot of say as to how that land gets dealt with…either leased or even sold eventually.''

''That's right,'' he said slowly. He set his drink down. ''What're you gettin' at, daughter?''

So she hadn't been as subtle as she'd hoped to be. She'd never been good at this kind of thing.

She may as well just get the matter out in the open. ''I was only wondering, Dad. What if you were to go to the town and return the lease on a few sections of that land to them—and then have the development group recommend leasing those sections to Ash. For him to ranch.''

At her suggestion, her father's chin snapped back in surprise—but not in anger, she was glad to note. It wasn't much, but it might be the thin edge she needed to get him to deal with Ash as a cattleman and businessman, if not as the man his daughter loved.

And she so wanted that for Ash! If she could bring her father around to endorsing the idea, so that Ash could start his own herd on land he might one day be able to buy, how could the rest of Rumor not follow suit and accept him back?

The only problem was, when Maura turned to Ash, she saw that his reaction went far beyond surprise, far beyond anger, even.

No, the look in his silver eyes was one of pure betrayal.

How had she known? Ash wondered wildly.

How had Maura known that he was putting the wheels in motion to do close to what she was suggesting? He knew better than to even think that Colby would have told anyone, but maybe Maura or her family knew Parnell Chapin. Sure, the businessman was all the way in Billings, but hell, the Kingsleys had probably done business at one time or another with every Tom, Dick and Harry in the state. Maybe the question was, what *didn't* the Kingsleys have a hand in?

Not that any of that mattered now. He'd caught the look on Stratton's face. There was no way Maura's father would consider subletting that land to him, much less recommend to his cronies in the development group that they endorse such a deal, not with Stratton feeling Ash had put his daughter up to it. He would just as soon cut one of his kids out of his will than sublease the land to the no-account cowboy clearly taking advantage of his daughter's affections by getting her to ask her daddy for a favor.

The very thought made Ash's own stomach turn.

And made him lash out. He shoved himself to his feet. "Dammit all, Maura, this is exactly what I asked you not to do. I don't want—or need—you to pull strings and finagle deals for me around town! Or persuade your daddy to do it, either!"

"But I'm not making the deal for you, Ash," she protested, her blue eyes huge with distress. She sprang to her feet as well, standing between him and her father, who continued to sit in silence, gazing from one to the other of them.

He's got to be loving this whole scene, Ash thought cynically.

Maura set her hand on his forearm in appeal. "I'm just...you know, putting the two of you together so you can discuss the matter. What you do is up to you—although I have no doubt you'll take advantage of the opportunity to let Dad know what a capable rancher you are, Ash. And I have every faith that you'll hear Ash out, Dad,'' she said, turning to her father.

"Well, there's nothin' to hear out, Stratton," Ash jumped in, needing in every way not to have Maura's father cut him dead. Ash shook off her hand and stepped around her. He wasn't about to be perceived as hiding behind her skirts either. "I'll be truthful and say that I have had it in mind to approach you at some point about that piece of land and yes, by God, give you a full accounting of my abilities and plans for it.''

Maura gasped. "You mean…you mean you were going to talk to Dad about that land?" she said.

"I was planning on it, once I got my affairs in order. But I'd as soon cut my own tongue out than ask him for anything now!"

Stratton frowned. "You'd've come to me knowing I'm about as fond of you as a bad case of hives?"

Ash crammed his fingers in the front pockets of his jeans. "Well, sure. You may not like me, and I may not be your biggest fan, either, but you're one of the smartest businessmen around, the evidence of which is just about everywhere a person can rest his eyes. And because of that, I felt I could've counted on you knowing a good deal when you saw one.''

His gut twisted in disappointment. "But that's not going to happen now.''

"Why can't it, Ash?" Maura asked. "It's what you'd planned to do…it's what you've wanted to do. Why?"

He turned to her, and it was all he could do not to respond, even after what she'd done, to the appeal in her eyes. He knew she'd only been trying to help him. But she needed to get a grip on those urges.

It would be the end of them both if she didn't.

"Sorry, Maura," he said. "I don't operate that way. I know you only wanted to help me, just like you want to help those kids down at the garden. But you know, there's just so much a body can do for another in this life. You can't make choices for people, and sometimes the best way to help them is just to stay the hell out of their business and let 'em take their knocks."

If her eyes had been huge before, now they were enormous.

Disgusted with himself for causing such a reaction in her, Ash grabbed his hat from where he'd set it on the TV. "I've got work to get back to, if you'll excuse me."

He crammed the Stetson on his head and figured, what did he have to lose? "Just one question, Stratton."

"What's that?"

"You say you're leasin' that land from Rumor to help the town out and to have in case of an emergency." He gestured to the outdoors beyond the window, where the leaves on the trees were so dangerously brown and dry they looked as if they'd crumble and blow away with the slightest breeze. "This drought is about the biggest emergency I can think of, yet you haven't put cattle on that land. Can I just ask why?"

At his question, Stratton's gaze became suddenly guarded. "I have my reasons," he said tersely.

Sure, Stratton was a smart businessman and damned good rancher, but in the end, blood was thicker than water. Ash would be ten kinds of fool to think Maura's father would give him any kind of break in this town—not so long as Rumor's bad seed was in danger of corrupting the rancher's daughter.

"Well, those reasons must be pretty damned good ones," Ash said, "'cause it doesn't make sense, not to me."

He grasped the doorknob. "Not that that's any measure. If you'll remember, I'm the rube who thought selling feed for Bob and Dave Brannigan was just the ticket I needed to get into ranching."

And he took his leave.

Maura stared at the door as if it held the explanation for what had just occurred.

"I don't understand it," she said, shaking her head slowly. How could things have turned so badly? How could she have been so wrong about how Ash would react?

It wasn't that she was completely unaware of the chance she took, bringing him and her father together. *And* trying to help Ash achieve his dream of having his own ranch when he had asked her not to.

"What don't you understand, little girl?" her father said with uncommon gentleness in his voice.

She turned to him. "I'm not saying Ash doesn't have a right to be upset with me. I guess I knew he would be. But he was so…so angry and frustrated that I didn't understand—that I couldn't understand—how he felt. And it's because I'm a Kingsley, who's never known a single disappointment or one minute of want!''

Her father's face was a study. She saw there all of his love for her, all of his own desire to help her, to protect her. And his realization of his limitation in doing that.

"Little girl," he began, then stopped. His mouth worked, as if he were trying to form words for which the thoughts hadn't yet gelled. "Maura. I love you with all of my heart, but that cowboy…Ash…is right. You gotta respect him for not wanting to be seen as tacking his ambitions on to your affections."

"Do *you* think he's doing that?" she asked fiercely, searching his face for reassurance. "Honestly, do you, Dad?"

Her father avoided her gaze. Stratton rose, shoving his fists into the pockets of his western-cut slacks. He contemplated his boot tops for a good minute.

"I don't now," he finally said. "But I don't think I'm the person that point matters to most in this situation."

He meant Ash—and what Ash believed.

That was the thing, because while he'd sounded certain, when talking in her bedroom, that her father would never cotton to an ex-con romancing his daughter, she knew she'd heard a sliver of hope in Ash's voice that overcoming adversity with honesty and conviction and hard work would win out in the end.

Yet too often life didn't work out that way, despite one's best efforts.

Maura hugged herself, feeling cold. "So have I botched this whole situation to the point where, even if you offered a deal to him for the land, Ash would never accept it, no matter the terms?''

''I can't answer that one, either, Maura.'' Still he avoided her gaze.

Her legs like rubber, Maura sat. What had she done? It had all made sense in her mind. And in her heart. When Ash and she had made love, she knew he had believed as she did in the future, in the power of their love for each other conquering anything that stood in the way of their happiness.

And she knew he loved her. He hadn't said the words, but that didn't matter. She knew.

But that love was only as strong as the trust between them, and hadn't she in a way just betrayed that trust?

She covered her face with her hands. ''Oh, Daddy.''

Maura felt the caress of her father's large hand on the crown of her head. ''What, Maura?''

''I...I want to be with Ash McDonough, Dad, more than I've ever wanted anything in my life,'' she said, tears clogging her throat. ''But how can I do that here in this town, where I'm Stratton Kingsley's daughter—and he's the bad seed of Rumor?''

''You've got your own dreams, though,'' he said reasonably, although she heard the slightest edge of worry in his voice. ''What about running your own ranch for those deserving kids? It's practically a done deal.''

''Yes,'' she said dully.

''And once you get into it and start seeing the kids blossom under your care, just like they were a bunch of those yellow marigolds in your garden, it'll seem worth it again.''

"I…I know. I get so much satisfaction from helping them. And from seeing how it helps Ash to lend his own brand of healing to them."

Maura lifted her head and looked at her father. "He's right, you know. He can bring them a perspective that I can't as someone who hasn't experienced that kind of disappointment in myself or those I love."

"I don't know," he said again. "Even so, that doesn't mean you shouldn't try and do what you *can* do for them. Many a time it will be more than enough, simply because you care and cared to try. You can't give up on those little ones."

His voice still held a degree of worry.

"Oh, I won't," Maura said. "I can't. I still want to help the children even more, with the comprehensive programs and activities I can provide on the ranch."

Her voice caught. And finally the tears spilled over. "But it wouldn't be the s-same without Ash."

"Aw, hon," Stratton said. He held out his arms, and Maura went into them without a moment's hesitation. Right now she needed the comfort of her father's embrace, to know the constancy of his love in this world of overwhelming uncertainty.

For she had not heard her father say that there was hope for Ash, either for her to help him or for Ash himself to put his past behind him and find redemption.

And if there was one thing she was certain of in this life, it *was* Stratton Kingsley's honesty.

Chapter Eight

Ash finally decided that he needed to join the rest of civilized society and pay a visit to MonMart. He knew of people who went there as part of their everyday lives and wouldn't hear a word said against it. And why not? The place had everything, from bakery to coffee shop to pharmacy to photo studio. Basically, what MonMart didn't have, the average person didn't need. He'd wager the sentiment was likely in the company's mission statement as set down by none other than Stratton Kingsley himself.

On this particular afternoon, Ash was in need of a book on starting your own corporation. Parnell Chapin had recommended he look into incorporating as a way of taking advantage of certain tax breaks available to ranchers.

That would be whenever another suitable tract of

land was found or became available. When Ash had informed the investor that he was no longer interested in pursuing those sections of land south of Rumor, Chapin had encouraged him not to abandon his dream of ranching his own spread. Not yet at least.

Ash picked up a book and flipped through it with little interest. It wasn't that he didn't want to work toward that goal, but reaching it had lost some of its urgency since the scene a few nights ago in Maura's apartment.

Realistically there wasn't much chance of him finding decent ranchland within shouting distance of Rumor—and it had to be here, because he'd meant what he said to Emmy about being here to stay. In fact, he'd become even more resolved since his conversation with Stratton, and Ash wasn't proud to admit that part of his reason for feeling so was out of sheer orneriness.

Just let him wonder whether the bad seed of Rumor is still kissing his daughter, Ash thought with some ruefulness, because the hell of it was, he *couldn't* leave Rumor—because of Maura. Even if he never found that piece of land that could be his, he wouldn't leave, not while there was even a breath of hope—hope she'd brought back to life within him, when he'd thought it dead and burned to ashes. Hope he now wished with all his might that he could snuff out for good, so he wouldn't be faced with the kind of torment that came with it.

Yes, that was certainly the hell of it.

Some impulse made Ash looked up to see a petite, handsome-looking older woman with short auburn hair across the table of books. She was thumbing through a novel by a bestselling mystery writer, and there was something about the tilt of her head that told him at once that he was looking at Maura's mother.

She had the same heart-shaped face, the same regal posture that seemed to be reinforced by the same backbone of steel. And for all that, the same uncommon grace.

She wasn't dressed extravagantly, he was somewhat surprised to note. She wore a pair of brushed-denim slacks in a shade of yellow that reminded him of a vibrant gold wheat field in the October sun. The sage-green shirt tucked into her slacks was rolled up at the sleeves and open at the collar. It was western casual in the way that celebrities who'd settled in Montana dressed, in clothes by that designer, Ralph Something-or-other.

Then she lifted her chin, and before Ash could turn away he was looking straight into cornflower-blue eyes that were exactly like Maura's. It kind of creeped him out, because there was the same knowing—or wanting to know—in her gaze that he'd never failed to see in Maura's.

The two of them measured each other for a long moment.

"You're Ash McDonough, aren't you?" she murmured.

He wondered how she'd guessed. Was it something in the way he looked or stood—as described to her by whom? And how had that person portrayed him?

He decided to assume the best. "Yes, ma'am, I am. And you've got to be Carolyn Kingsley."

Her delicate eyebrows rose. "Indeed," she said, apparently the refined version of his own use of *really*. The tone was exactly the same.

"Pleased to meet you." He reached across the table to offer his hand. Hers was small, like her daughter's, in his.

"You're certainly a handsome devil," she observed with a wry smile. "I can see why my daughter became smitten. She speaks highly of you, you know. So does my nephew's wife, Jilly."

He touched the edge of his index finger to the brim of his Stetson to hide his quick swallow to dislodge the emotional lump in his throat. "I'm humbled by their praise, ma'am."

"Be sure that you deserve it."

He was about to reply when she nodded toward the book in his hand. "Are you starting your own business?" she asked.

Ash stiffened. Damn, he'd forgotten he still held the how-to book. "I'm thinkin' about it," he said, hedging.

"You must know."

"Pardon?"

"Well, either you are or you aren't." She actually sniffed. "Saying you're thinking about it makes you seem a man who's unsure of what he wants."

Ash was at a loss as how to respond. She got all that from a simple *I'm thinking about it?*

At his apparent blank look, she sighed. "Take it from me, Ash. Don't be hesitant about stating straight out what you believe in—or what you want out of life. You'll gain more respect that way, no matter how pie-in-the-sky those goals may seem to the uneducated observer.''

She went on sagely, "Just be certain that you truly want what you say you do. Enough to fight against all odds to get it.''

Ash nodded. Her advice definitely held an underlying message that was specific to him. And despite his cynical state of mind, he was compelled to deliver a message of his own.

"I'm not the bad seed your husband and the rest of Rumor believe me to be,'' he said. "I made some big mistakes, but I paid for 'em.''

Now Carolyn nodded. "Stratton has his opinions, to be sure. But neither is he rigid in them. If you're in earnest about our daughter, he's bound to see it and come around—'' the sliver of a smile touched her lips "—eventually.''

Then that smile died and her blue eyes turned frosty as she looked him dead in the eye. "If you're not, however, you'll deal not only with him but with me. And you don't want that to happen, young man, I assure you.''

He returned her gaze steadily. "I believe you.''

He'd always believed Maura had gotten her stubbornness and the steel in her backbone from Stratton. He'd been wrong. Clearly, behind every strong man stood a strong woman.

So what else could he have been wrong about when it came to Stratton Kingsley? Ash wondered.

"If I might ask a question, ma'am,'' he said abruptly. "How did you know who I was?''

"Seriously?" She appraised him. "You don't look as if you belong here."

"Meaning?"

"Ash, I have four sons. Each is as different and as alike—and as familiar—as standing on the top of a rise and looking in four directions at the Montana landscape. And my boys have all gone in their different directions while still staying close to home."

She dropped her gaze, ostensibly to study her immaculate manicure. "Maura on the other hand—she's got a bit of me in her. I came from the East Coast, you see, and it was to make a life with the man I loved. Where he was, that was my home, where *I* belonged."

"But I do belong here. I was born in these parts and lived here all my life," Ash said, puzzled, "until…well, you know."

"As has Maura. But she belongs here just as you belong here…only if you have a purpose in staying. Maura is searching for that purpose, and whether it'll be this community garden or the ranch for children who simply need love and attention more than anything—or you—has yet to be seen. But she'll go where her heart is. And when all's said and done, so will you."

Ash still had little clue as to what Carolyn meant, but it was clear he wouldn't get the chance to ask when she slapped shut the book she held, punctuating the end of the conversation.

"Well!" she said with a devastatingly captivating smile that had no doubt brought the great and powerful Stratton Kingsley to his knees on more than one occasion. Ash knew, because it was Maura's smile. "I've got to be going. It was interesting—and nice—to finally meet you, Ash.''

"And you, too," he murmured, for she had already turned to go. "And you, too."

"We're *planting* the bulbs, Diego," Maura said as she rushed to the front flower bed in the community garden. "Not eating them."

The six-year-old, a black-haired child with the most soulful brown eyes Maura had ever seen in a child, made a face as, her warning too late, his tongue encountered what had to be one bitter daffodil bulb.

"Here you go, dear, spit it out now, quickly," she said, cupping under his chin the half-used paper towel she pulled from her apron pocket.

The boy dutifully spit, then looked up at her. "That din't taste nothin' like an onion!" he exclaimed.

She peered down at him in puzzlement. "Why would you think it might?"

"'Cause it looked like the onion bulbs we planted in the spring and then dug up at the harvest. I just wondered if they tasted as good goin' in the ground as they did comin' out."

Maura exchanged a private glance with DeeDee, who had come up behind Diego, but averted her eyes when it became clear both women would need to devote their complete attention to suppressing their laughter.

"I'm sorry I wasn't keeping an eye on him, Maura," DeeDee said after clearing her throat a few times. "I needed a hand from Parker to help me with the third-graders mulching the other bed."

"Don't worry," Maura said. "There's no harm done that a juice box can't fix."

She clasped her hands in front of her. "So, Diego. What did we learn just now?"

"Daffodils ain't for eatin'," he answered emphatically. "O' course, that's how I felt 'bout onions till you got me to taste 'em."

The two women laughed, unable to resist the urge this time, as Maura drew the dear little boy against her side for a hug.

Then the sound of more feminine laughter joined theirs. Maura turned to see Valerie Fairchild a few yards away.

"Val!" she exclaimed, walking quickly to her side and taking the other woman's hands in hers, Maura's gaze searching Val's face for signs of stress. Maura had heard rumors of the difficulties the veterinarian might be dealing with right now.

"I'm so happy to see you!" Maura told her with warm sincerity. "What brings you to the garden?"

Val returned the squeeze of her hands. "Your rescued fawn, Smokey. We thought the children might like to meet him before he leaves."

"The fawn's going somewhere?" Maura asked in mild alarm.

"Somewhere safe, where he'll be happy," said a masculine voice from behind her.

Maura turned—and there he was. Ash. She'd suffered a thousand agonies since the evening two days before in her apartment. She'd been deathly afraid he wouldn't come back to the garden. That he would never want to see her again.

But here he was. And the look in his gray eyes as he drank her in—part gladness at seeing her, part self-reproach that he couldn't prevent that reaction—made her own reaction as mixed.

He gave the fawn, whom he held on a lead, a calming pat on the neck. "Val's been in contact with the DNR ever since we brought her Smokey to nurse to health," he said. "Apparently up in northwest Montana there's some good places where a half-grown deer will be able to integrate into an existing herd."

"It s-sounds perfect for him," Maura murmured with a catch in her throat. She would miss the visits to the enclosure behind Val's clinic, where Smokey had been able to mend from the last of the effects of the forest fire.

At least the physical ones. Who knew whether the fawn would take to life in the wild again. One could only hope—and pray—that he would survive and thrive.

She considered it as good a sign as any that the fawn's black nose trembled not so much in fear as in curiosity when Ash knelt on one knee, his arm looped around the young deer's neck, to both calm and control Smokey so the children could pet him. He'd lost some of his white spots as he'd matured, but it would be several months before the velvety knobs between his ears would grow to antlers.

Yes, he had been one of the lucky ones, for the fire still raged across south-central Montana, destroying more vegetation and wildlife than Maura could begin to contemplate. It gave her a sick feeling every time she thought about it. Neither she nor Ash had been called back to fight the fire, their close brush with disaster earning them down time for the rest of the season. Yet Maura knew from her brother Reed's reports that its ferocity hadn't abated, and the crews were growing weary.

Her thoughts tempered her enjoyment of the charming sight of one little girl who, madly sucking her thumb, leaned back against Ash's legs in timidity as he guided her hand over Smokey's smooth brown fur.

"See?" he murmured. "I told you he wouldn't hurt you. He's as gentle as can be. He knows what it's like to be hurt, and he wouldn't do that to someone else."

Big brown eyes gazed up at him solemnly, and then around the thumb a smile formed as the child nodded. "Soft," she said.

The other children weren't as shy, and Ash had to caution them to speak softly and pet Smokey gently as he told them the fawn's story, just like the legend of Smokey the Bear.

"It's funny how fascinated they are with him, because most of these kids have surely seen the deer foraging in the areas around Rumor," Maura said to Val as they watched the scene. "I mean, I've had to entirely enclose the garden in six-foot-high wire mesh to keep the local fauna—deer, rabbits and raccoons, not to mention the crows—from munching away at the veggies. Especially this year, with the fire eating up all their food," she added softly.

Val nodded solemnly. "Still, most children rarely get the chance to see a wild animal like this up close. It's a wonderful educational experience for them."

Chin lowered, Maura clasped her hands behind her

back. "I'd heard, Val, that you might be dealing with breast cancer."

"Ah, the good old rumor mill—and I don't mean our esteemed newspaper," she said, her voice tinged with wry tolerance. "With a network like the one in this town, who needs the World Wide Web?"

"I'm so sorry." Maura knew little about the quiet, reserved veterinarian. Val was from the East Coast, which amazed Maura. She herself loved Montana, but choosing to make the state one's home—and electing to have Rumor as one's address—without a compelling reason seemed a little mad, even among people who had garnered a reputation for being so. As the saying went, one didn't have to be crazy to live here, but it definitely helped.

"I know the situations are not the same at all, but my father's lung cancer has been in remission for five years now," Maura said. "Every day people are beating cancer. You will, too, I just know it."

"Thanks, Maura. If anything it's the support of friends and family that's going to make the difference. My sister Jinni is here now, which helps so much. The surgeon feels pretty confident that the lumpectomy successfully got all of the malignancy. I started chemo just this week." She nodded firmly. "The prognosis is good. Very good."

But it still had to be a terrifying time for her, Maura thought. "You know that if there's any way I or my family can help, we're there for you," she murmured, giving Val's hand another empathetic squeeze.

"Thank you. Everyone's been wonderful with their support."

Yes, the people of Rumor could be as warm and accepting as they were cold and rejecting, often with no middle ground.

The children's fascination with Smokey didn't seem to wane as the afternoon did, so at half past five Maura announced that the petting zoo was closed for the day. In any case, it was time for the kids to get home to supper.

In the bustle of loading Smokey into Val's trailer and seeing to the cleanup of tools, Maura didn't realize she was alone in the garden until she put the lock on the shed door and turned around.

Alone, that was, except for Ash.

He stood on the other side of the garden between two vegetable plots, his fingers crammed into the front pockets of his jeans, his Stetson pulled low over his eyes. In the fading light, his face was thrown into relief, making him seem as much a mystery to her as ever.

She stood for a moment just drinking him in. And praying that she would know how to handle the situation between them. She honestly wanted what was best for Ash…for both of them. *Please. Please let me do what's right.*

"I didn't know if you'd come back to the garden," Maura finally said. "I was so afraid my actions the other night had driven you away for good."

His mouth twisted. "I guess I've no one to blame but myself for feeling hurt that you could think I'd've shirked my responsibility here. I told the kids I'd come as often as I could till the garden was closed for the winter. I'd never go back on my promise to them.

These kids have had enough disappointment and in-consistency in their lives.''

He glanced away, then back to her again. ''And be-sides, I told you I'd be here. No matter what happened between us, I'd never go back on that promise, either.''

Her throat tightened with emotion. ''I...I guess I knew that, in my heart.''

She wanted to pour that heart out to him right now, wanted him to understand her as she had tried with all her might to understand him.

''Ash...I'm sorry for what happened at my apart-ment. I didn't know what you'd been planning.''

His mouth twisted more. ''Or you wouldn't have tried to pull some strings for me?''

''Yes. No! I mean, when we talked, you know, after making love, it seemed to me that you might have come around some to thinking my dad could deal with you fairly and might back a proposal for you to ranch the widow's property, which seemed like a great option for you.''

Her fingers twisted around themselves. ''I mean, it was already clear the city council wants to make use of it, giving me the right to run my ranch there.''

He made a sound of exasperation. ''You're com-pletely naive if you think being Stratton Kingsley's daughter didn't have a whole lot to do with that.''

''What if it did!'' she asked, her own exasperation flaring. ''It doesn't mean that either the city council or the development group would never be open to pro-posals from others on how to use the land.''

''Oh, I think they'd consider any reasonable plan—just not from the drug-dealing ex-con their most influential member would just as soon have out of his daughter's life.''

''But you were never a drug dealer! Why do you persist in calling yourself that?''

''Because I might as well be, in the eyes of everyone in Rumor. After all, it's what I was convicted of. And even if I didn't deal drugs, I spent five years doing hard time—and that's not the kind of experience that people pass off as providing a little object lesson.''

''Stop it, Ash!'' Maura pulled off her canvas gardening gloves and shoved them, fingers first, into the back pocket of her jeans. ''Stop treating me and everyone else like sheltered nuns without any real life experience. You assume I can never, ever understand what you went through, what you felt, the devastation to your spirit. I believe I can understand, Ash.''

She pointed north, toward the part of town that, had there been railroad tracks, would have been the wrong side of them. It was where Ash grew up.

''I can understand you. And the children out there who need help with the situations they've faced and are facing,'' she said. ''No matter what the situation is, whether it's an alcoholic parent or losing a mother or father through divorce or death, or living with the stress of not enough food to eat or the lack of a roof over their head, it's their *world,* and in that world everything's as urgent as your ordeals.''

She lifted her chin defiantly. ''I understand *that,* and that's what makes the difference. And because of that, I'll never stop trying to understand better, understand more, whatever it takes to help them.''

At her passionate speech, he took a step toward her,

his blood clearly running high, as well. "God, you're stubborn! I've never faulted you, Maura, for trying to help these kids any way you can. But I'm not one of them."

"You mean, with you the damage is already done and you're a hopeless case? The mistakes are irreversible and the consequences everlasting?" she said rather recklessly, knowing that, in a way, she was playing with fire. Yet she wasn't about to pussyfoot around him or his problem any longer.

She stalked a few steps forward, pointing at him this time. "You think I don't understand that's what you mean—"

"You don't, Maura," Ash said.

"—but I do," she went on as if she hadn't been interrupted. "I just don't happen to share your resignation that redemption is impossible. It's never too late, Ash."

She slashed her arm through the air between them. "Never."

He stared at her for a long while, his gray eyes like ice—not cold and chilling but icicle sharp, penetrating her gaze. Maura gave as good as she got. He would never convince her that she was wrong, believing that even when a fire's damage had been its most encompassing, the ashes their coldest, that there could not be new life. That there could not be hope.

Whatever he saw in her eyes made him eventually turn away from her. He took several steps deeper into the garden, and she had to shade her eyes not to lose him. The sun was setting now—a September sun whose angle was sharp, the light uncommonly blinding.

"He came to my house to get me because I missed the hearing to set the trial date," Ash said, his back to her.

His comment was so out of the blue that it took a moment for Maura to figure out who "he" was: the sheriff's deputy.

So—Ash was finally going to tell her what happened that day. She wanted to take it as a good sign, but something in his demeanor sent an arrow of trepidation through her.

She waited on tenterhooks for him to go on.

"I was out on bail," he said, his voice eerily devoid of emotion or inflection. "Mom had been able to scrape together enough to make bond so I didn't have to sit in jail during my trial, but it'd maxed us out. There was literally no money, no resources left. That day…we'd taken her to the doctor."

He dropped his chin, which muffled his voice so that Maura had to strain to hear him. "He told her that the chemo hadn't worked. The cancer had spread, in fact, gone into her liver and her brain and…and…"

Emotion entered his voice with a vengeance as he rasped, "There was hardly a place inside her it wasn't eatin' her alive."

Maura pressed her hand over her mouth to keep from gasping in pure sympathy. She had a feeling that she was hearing Ash tell this story for the first time— a story that no one knew outside of his family, not even Jilly.

"We brought her home. I had to carry her into the

house she was so weak. All I knew at that moment was that I couldn't leave her,'' Ash said. "Of course I was aware that the hearing was going on and that missing it was going to put me into a worse position than I already was in. I tried calling the lawyer I'd been assigned, and all I got was an answering machine. I even called the court clerk's office, asking the woman on the other end to get a message to him. She said she'd try but they were shorthanded that day.''

Ash took another aimless step away from her. "Apparently she didn't, because an hour later the deputy knocked at the door. When he said he'd come to take me away, I told him I needed some time—just until the next day or so, until I knew Mom had gotten past the first shock. But he wouldn't listen. He said he had a warrant."

Ash swallowed audibly. "I pleaded with him. 'Just a few more hours, then.''' He gestured with his hand, just as he might have done when talking to the deputy. "'Think about your own mother,' I said.''

His hand dropped. "But he wouldn't listen. He said the hearing had been too important to miss, no matter the circumstances, and I ought to've known that.''

Maura had an inkling that Ash was indeed back in his mother's living room reliving that awful episode—and she had pushed him to go there.

"So what happened?'' she asked with the utmost gentleness.

"He said he had to take me in. When he grabbed my arm, I guess I went a little crazy. It was like what had happened in the past six months came to a head inside me, and I realized how little control I had over anything—most of all my mom's cancer. And so I laid into him with everything I had in me.''

He gave what under other circumstances might have been called a rueful laugh. The sound was devoid of mirth, however. ''At seventeen I was no runt, but this guy was a lot bigger than me, stronger and better trained. Still, it took him more than a few tries to wrestle me to the floor to subdue me. And yes, I got in a few good punches, by sheer luck more than anything, if you can call it luck. Bloodied his nose so that, right in front of Mom and Emmy, he hauled off and hit me in the face—twice. Gave me a split lip and a shiner, before shoving my face into the floor and kneeing me in the kidney so he could handcuff me.''

His shoulders slumped. His voice fell to a whisper. ''He'd've done worse if my mother hadn't dragged herself off the sofa through some superhuman effort and held on to his sleeve. And begged his mercy for her son.''

He said nothing else for a long moment, then Ash sighed and tipped his head back as he stared at the purpling sky. ''So now you know the worst,'' he said.

''Know what?'' Maura asked. What had he revealed that was worse than what she already perceived she'd known?

''That it wasn't all the innocent mistake of a gullible teenager,'' he said with some impatience. ''I deliberately struck a peace officer. I couldn't stop myself. And in doing that, I wronged my family most of all. It was one thing for Mom and Emmy to know I was being tried for dealing drugs—a charge that up to then I'd intended to fight because I was innocent of any intentional crime, and I had hope of the court taking that into account. But it was another thing altogether to be treated like a criminal in front of my mother and sister, this time for a crime I *did* commit—with them witness to the whole awful scene.''

And where earlier his voice had swum with emotion, now it held a dearth of it as he revealed, ''I'll never forgive myself for that, even if both Mom and Emmy can. Never.''

Maura's throat ached with unshed tears of compassion. What would she have done if someone had come to take her away when her father had been diagnosed with cancer? She wouldn't have left his side, either, would have fought with all her might to stay.

''I'm so sorry, Ash,'' she whispered, and she was surprised to feel a wetness on her cheeks as the tears spilled over. ''I'm so sorry.''

''Yeah, I'm sorry, too, Maura. Because the problem is, it doesn't change a thing between us.''

He turned his head, his face in profile. ''Y'see, the deputy I assaulted was Dave Reingard.''

Maura blinked in confusion. ''Dave Reingard? DeeDee's husband?''

''The same.''

She was still confused, not by the name but the significance of it that Ash felt she couldn't comprehend.

''Well, he could have shown you some leniency, given the extenuating circumstances,'' Maura said stoutly. ''I think the fact that he's now in prison for murder speaks for itself.''

''That's exactly my point.'' Still Ash remained half turned from her, as if he couldn't look her in the eye, and Maura knew suddenly that it wasn't because he didn't want to reveal himself to her, but that he didn't want to see in her eyes that she couldn't accept what he revealed.

"Don't you see, Maura?" he said. "Dave Reingard's in prison for a crime that will brand him and his family for the rest of their lives—brand them by everyone in this town, including you."

Chapter Nine

Maura noticed only then that they'd stood several feet apart while he told his story. It was a separation on his part, an isolation that she knew was as deliberate as it was unconscious. Because she couldn't know what it was like to be in his shoes. To be branded.

"You and Dave Reingard—you're not the same. Not the same at all," Maura said stubbornly.

"Even if we aren't, it doesn't change things between *us*, does it?" Ash's chin fell to his chest as if he'd grown too weary to hold his head up any longer. "You're still the rancher's daughter, a princess of Rumor royalty with everything going for her and everything to look forward to. And I'm the ex-con who's faced with fighting for every bit of respectability he can get. Hell, the only thing royal about me is how I screwed up."

"I can't help being a Kingsley!" she said in frustration, more with herself than him. "And I won't apologize for it, for using the advantages and resources I've been blessed with to help others."

"You shouldn't apologize, Maura." He turned at last to face her. His features were haggard, his eyes, even in the burgeoning light, a dull gray, revealing a spirit that was spent. "What you do for these kids— what you do here in the garden and what you're trying to provide for them with the ranch is just about as fine a thing as one person can do for another. You only have to look around to see how much being a part of the garden means to them, and how without being able to come here during the winter…it's going to be like them going dormant, just a little bit. Because it's your spirit and love and support that's helping these kids most, Maura."

He shook his head slowly. "But I can't be one of them, Maura. I can't be one of your fix-it projects."

"I've *never* considered you—or them—that way, Ash," Maura choked out. "And it's not me that's the problem. Sure, you caught a tough break and made it ten times worse out of anger and fear. At seventeen you were put in the impossible position of choosing whether to leave your mother when she needed you most or make it to a hearing for a crime you never committed, and I have nothing but compassion for that young man, Ash."

Her voice cracked. "It's time you did, too, and put it behind you for good so you can see how you've got everything to live for. And if you're too pigheaded to do that, so you can take advantage of the opportunities that have been put at *your* disposal, then you're not the man I believed you to be.''

"Well, that's your problem to deal with," Ash answered. "I've never pretended to be anything other than what I am—the rebel ex-con with both feet planted firmly in reality. I'm resigned to the fact that I'm going to have to pull myself up by my bootstraps, and that it's gonna take one incredible effort. And I won't drag you down with me any more than I'd let you give me a hand up.''

He squinted at the setting sun, as if reckoning time by it. "I've gotta go.''

She didn't want him to leave like this. Maura reached out to catch him by the arm just as he turned to go. When she grasped air instead, she stumbled over a piece of edging. Down to her hands and knees in the dirt she went.

Ash was instantly kneeling at her side. "Maura! Are you all right?" He took her elbow to help her sit back on her heels.

"Yes." She brushed her palms together.

She lifted her chin to find their faces were inches apart. Heat radiated from him—that oh-so-familiar heat that always seemed to take her by surprise after having him behave so standoffishly.

His gaze was hungry, and she suspected hers was, too. It was so intimate there in the garden, with dusk falling and just a hint of chill in the air. She wanted him to kiss her, but knew that doing so would tear him up inside.

She should get up, move away, let him have his precious distance, let him push her away once and for all and prove himself right: that the obstacles between them were too great to be overcome. That all hope was lost.

Something rose up in her in rebellion, and instead of moving away Maura said, "I love you, Ash."

He closed his eyes, shutting her out without moving a muscle. "Ah, Maura," he said raggedly. "Don't. Don't love me. You were right, you know—when you said you would never be swayed from going after happiness. And you do deserve every happiness, without giving up any of it in the process."

Opening his eyes, he looked at her sadly. "And you would be giving it up, with me."

"I wouldn't, Ash!" She pushed up off her heels and grasped his shoulders, purely exasperated. Purely desperate. How was it that she came to be in this position of begging this man to love her?

"We can both find happiness, if you'd just believe you could," she said. She actually shook him, and he grasped her waist to keep his balance. "Ash, we love each other! Oh, I know you haven't said it, but you do. I know you do. And as long as we have that, the only thing we lack is believing in that love! Once you believe that we're meant to be together, honestly, Ash, the rest will fall into place."

His gaze dropped, and she knew him well enough by now that it was not out of avoidance but a compulsion—to focus on her lips.

"It's not that simple," he said, but his voice lacked its earlier conviction.

"It *is* that simple," she contradicted softly, wrapping her arms around his neck. Almost reflexively, his fingers tightened on her waist. "I'm not saying things won't be hard at times, that there won't be some bumps along the way. What relationship, what life, doesn't have its challenges to overcome? But we face those challenges together. Not apart. Not alone."

She lifted her chin a fraction, so that all he had to do was breathe to kiss her. "That's what I'm trying to tell *you,* Ash McDonough. I'm not trying to make you a fix-it project. I'm trying to make you realize that you have every resource within you to be successful. To be happy."

She took a deep breath herself, bringing her breasts in contact with his chest. Ash groaned.

"And the best part is, you don't have to do it by yourself," she whispered. "Not anymore."

"It isn't that simple," he stubbornly maintained. "It'll never be that simple…"

His mouth on hers was warm and not at all gentle, as if he could not get enough of her. She didn't care that the stubble of his beard scratched her skin. She wanted him as badly. He sat back on his heels, pulling her with him, and she wrapped her legs around his waist as she'd done once before, knowing it would make him growl with pleasure. He did not disappoint.

"Maura," he said against her lips, his breath as hot as his kiss. "What you do to me."

"I know, I know," she whispered, letting her head fall back as he one-handedly undid the first few buttons on her workshirt before pressing his mouth to the slope of her breast above her bra.

"Yes," she gasped. "Yes, this—*this* is what matters, Ash. Not that I'm a Kingsley or that you're an ex-con.''

His mouth moved lower, the caress of his mouth intimate, branding, bringing her to life, setting her on fire. She grasped his Stetson by the brim and tossed it aside so she could cradle his head against her, dying inside to know him more completely through this connection that had always obliterated all doubt and uncertainty.

"And you're right, it's not money or power that makes dreams come true," she murmured. "It's people. People working together."

She dug her fingers into this thick dark hair and dragged his head up so she could look him in the eyes. "We could do it—build the children's ranch for me, the cattle ranch for you, make them one and the same—on our own. Let's do it. Let's get away from Rumor, go somewhere else in Montana and make a life together."

His eyes…oh, his eyes were so deep and rich and tormented as he gazed at her, his face a map of crossroads and conflicts that she wondered if they'd ever lead home.

"Leave Rumor? Is that what it would take?" he asked hoarsely. "Making you leave everyone you love?"

"I'm not choosing between you and them. They'll still be here. They'll still love me as much as I love them."

She tried to pull him close again, to reestablish the connection between them, but he resisted, gripping her upper arms and holding her away from him.

''Leave Rumor,'' he repeated, his voice rough with momentary longing. ''God, you don't know how much right now I'd love to shake the dust of this confounded town off my boots and never look back. But that wouldn't work for you, Maura. You're a Kingsley, and no amount of distance is gonna change that. Your family is who you are, what makes you happy.''

He took her face between his hands. ''How could I stand being the man who took you away from them? If I were them, I'd hate that man, too. Besides, leaving won't change who I am, either. And if I'm bound to stay, the problem is,'' he whispered, touching his forehead to hers with great weariness, ''giving you up may be the only way I can do what I set out to do when I returned to Rumor.''

''No!'' Maura cried softly. He couldn't be right! She pressed her cheek against his. ''There's got to be a way, Ash. Some way that we can be together…''

Abruptly, a beam of light illuminated them where they knelt. ''McDonough.''

Maura gasped in surprise, then in shock at the descriptive oath Ash muttered vehemently near her ear. He gripped her waist to lift her off of his lap, then hauled himself to his feet, giving her a hand up, too, before shoving her behind him. She figured out why when she looked down and saw her gaping shirt.

She quickly did up the buttons and ran her fingers through her hair. It would still be pretty obvious to anyone who cared to notice that she and Ash had been deeply involved with each other. His own hair was mussed on the sides where she'd run her fingers through it, and one shirttail hung outside his jeans.

"Sheriff Tanner," Ash said as calmly as if he'd met the man going into church. "Fancy meeting you here."

Maura peeked around his shoulder to see that indeed, Holt Tanner stood on the other side of the flower bed with a man she didn't know.

"Hello, Holt," she said with nary a quaver in her voice.

He shifted the flashlight to her face, momentarily blinding her. "Maura Kingsley, is that you?"

She shaded her eyes. "Yes. Is there something I can help you with?"

He said nothing in reply, but he fairly radiated disapproval—although it wasn't directed at her. Instead, Holt's gimlet gaze was trained on Ash.

"I've come lookin' for you, McDonough." He chucked his thumb in the direction of the man at his side. "This here is your new parole officer, Tom Carter. But you'd actually know that right now if you'd made your appointment with him at the diner half an hour ago."

She saw Ash close his eyes in self-reproach.

"I won't lie to you, Sheriff," he said. "I plain forgot."

"Ash was helping me with the children here in the garden," Maura said. "He'd brought the fawn whose life he saved—as well as saving mine—for the kids to pet, and I kept him afterward to talk. So please, let me take the blame for making him late—"

"Not at all, Sheriff," Ash said, interrupting, and she could tell he wasn't happy at having to do so. "The blame's all on me, make no mistake."

Holt didn't exactly look appeased in any case, but

he didn't argue the point, either. "Well, it's going to cost you a trip to the courthouse to straighten this out, McDonough."

"Fine. Whatever it takes." Ash turned to the other man. "It won't happen again, Mr. Carter, I can promise you that."

"I hope not," the parole officer said, his perusal going from Ash's tousled hair to his rumpled shirt to the Stetson that still lay brim up in the dirt. "You're a few months from being free. It wouldn't do to let yourself get distracted and mess up a clean record."

Maura felt Ash's arm tense then, as if by great effort, relax again. "No, sir."

He stooped to pick up his hat, thumping it against his thigh before setting it firmly on his head. "Well, let's get going. My pickup's right over there. Lead the way."

The sheriff shook his head. "Sorry, McDonough. I'm going to have to ask you to ride in the county car."

If Ash had tensed up before, now Maura could see him turn to pure granite. "I can't follow you in my pickup?"

"'Fraid not. Department policy."

He looked about to argue, then he dropped his chin in a single nod. How humiliating this had to be for him! Maura thought. It was so reminiscent of that time with his mother.

"Do you want me to come, Ash?" she asked, setting her hand on his arm. "I could follow in my SUV—"

"No!" he said curtly, then more gently, "Just… no."

He wouldn't look at her, and too late she realized

that she had tried to fix things again, when he wanted her to let him handle things alone.

"A-all right, Ash," Maura whispered.

It was if he were deliberately ignoring her as he turned and walked, Holt Tanner and his parole officer on either side of him, to the sheriff's car. Ash opened one of the rear doors and got in as Holt and Tom Carter slid into the two front seats.

In the next moment they were gone. And in the dwindling light of an exhausted day, it was Maura who was alone.

Ash entered Handy Andy's Hardware on the jingle of the bell overhead. He noticed immediately that it had an eerie effect on the various and sundry clientele.

They all turned as one and stared at him stone-faced.

Momentarily taken aback, Ash paused with his hand on the door handle. Not that he expected a ticker-tape parade, but Rumorites on the whole had been generally civil since his return.

Today might prove the exception. Ash wasn't acquainted with some of the folk, but it didn't seem to matter. An elderly man, apparently on the hunt for a handle to attach to the plunger in his hand, fairly glared at him before going back to the plumbing section. In a rare occurrence, the Missuses Alden and Raymond had evidently un-Velcroed themselves from their perennial seats at the Calico Diner to take in the action at Andy's.

The two ladies' mouths were pursed so tight it looked as if they'd taken a dose of alum. They glowered at Ash for a long moment before putting their gray heads together and whispering behind upheld hands.

Even Andy himself, whom Ash had always found ready with a joke or at least a cordial greeting, avoided Ash's gaze with the studiousness of a monk.

Ash didn't usually come into town midday unless, like today, he was in the middle of a job that required some piece of equipment or supply that the Holmes shop happened to be lacking. On this occasion it was a pump vital in supplying precious water to the herd.

Ash shrugged off the cold climate in the hardware store as best he could and transacted his business quickly before going on to another couple of errands at the gas station and post office. He got the same frosty reception there, though, and he was beginning to think he had dropped into the Stepford version of Rumor when he spied DeeDee Reingard rushing toward him down the sidewalk on Main Street.

"Well, DeeDee, I'll admit to being glad to see a friendly face," he quipped. The smile died on his lips when he saw her anxious expression.

"What is it, DeeDee?" Ash asked.

She pulled him off the sidewalk to a space between the post office and drugstore. Then she just stood there for a few moments looking up at him, her eyes full of empathy and indignation.

"What a bunch of busybodies this town has!" she finally said on a huff. "Heaven forbid people would mind their own business!"

At her words he experienced a moment of uneasiness that he tamped down. No reason to borrow trouble.

"Is there something goin' on?" he asked. "I noticed I can't seem to get even a polite nod from people today."

DeeDee pressed her lips together, obviously at odds about what to say. Then she blew the air out. "Ash, I'd give anything not to be the one to tell you this."

The uneasiness reared up. "Just say it, DeeDee."

"It's all over town that you got caught seducing Maura Kingsley last night in her garden," she said, the disgust in her voice obvious for having to have this conversation. "They say...they say you've been using the fact that you saved her life in the forest fire to get her to associate with you. So that you could take advantage of her."

Ash swore under his breath. *He knew it.* He knew that it would only be a matter of time before the townspeople would find some way to turn a good deed into a bad one—by the bad seed of Rumor. Damn this town and its judgmental ways!

And damn himself. He should have stayed away from Maura from the beginning. It wasn't going to do his reputation any good, and it was only going to cause Maura strife with those who cared for her and wanted to protect her.

"I can't believe Holt Tanner would have been telling such tales, so who was it that put this particular kernel of gossip out there for everybody and their brother to come take a peck at?" he asked.

"That new parole officer of yours must have gone to supper at the diner last night. Being a stranger in town, I'm sure someone got to chatting with him to find out why he was here in Rumor." DeeDee pushed her bangs off her forehead impatiently. "Who knows if he meant to cause a stir, but that was all it took."

"Of course." Ash's own impatience was at an all-time high. "I don't know why a thousand firefighters have been risking their lives in the Custer Forest when there's a wildfire of gossip spreading through this town that needs to be snuffed out good and proper."

DeeDee gazed up at him, her face drawn. "That's not the worst of it, Ash. People are not just blaming you, they're blaming Maura, too, saying she should know better than to let an ex-con work around children."

She bit her lower lip in sheer misery. "They're saying she's not a proper role model for them—and that she ought not to be given the money and land to run a ranch for kids. And that she should be fired from running the garden."

Ash rocked back on his heels as DeeDee dropped yet another bombshell. "The Rumor Development Group has called a special meeting tonight to review the situation and decide what to do. Members of the city council are coming, too, to listen to what the group says—and to decide about the community garden."

His heart felt as if a hand squeezed it in a death grip. He had to admit that *this*…this he never saw coming. Fine, if the town wanted to treat him like a pariah. But he'd never suspected they'd cut one of their own—one of their best—in the process.

He expected to pay for his sins; he hadn't thought about how others would pay for them, too.

And that had been his fatal mistake—again.

Everything he touched he tainted, it seemed. If

Maura lost this opportunity due to him, he didn't know what he'd do.

There was only one way to ensure she didn't, Ash realized.

"Is Maura down at the garden?" he asked DeeDee urgently.

She frowned in concern. "You might want to cut a swath around her for a while there, Ash, till things die down—"

"I need to find her now!" he interrupted.

DeeDee hesitated, then nodded. "I saw Stratton and her heading into the Calico not ten minutes ago."

So Maura was with her father. Ash didn't relish facing Stratton right now. It would be just like the rancher to call him out. Of course, it wasn't that Ash didn't think Stratton wouldn't have had good reason in this instance, or that Ash himself might be better off dead.

"Well, I guess if I'm gonna make a statement," Ash told DeeDee grimly, "that'd be the way it'd make the most impact."

He shrugged, ready for once to play the part of the bad seed for all it was worth. He had to. For Maura.

But he knew what he should never have done in the first place: come back to Rumor, Montana.

Maura raised her chin to find her father considering her thoughtfully across the Formica tabletop of the booth at the Calico Diner.

"Not hungry, darlin'?" Stratton asked. He'd insisted that they have lunch today in this most public of settings. A Kingsley didn't tuck tail and hide. Especially when she'd done nothing wrong.

Oh sure, her judgment hadn't been the best, and while that was hardly a hanging offense, she'd had ample insight into Ash's world to know that that fact alone could be just as damning in this town.

If she hadn't been acquainted with how he felt before, she sure enough was now.

"Not really," she belatedly answered her father. "And for once it has nothing to do with the fact that my order is wrong." She tried a wan smile, acutely aware of the other patrons, who for the most part were admirably managing not to stare. "I guess I'm worried about the meeting tonight."

"I know. But I'll be there for every minute of the discussion, even if I'm not allowed to vote on account of your being my daughter."

His large hand covered hers on the tabletop. "Your mother'll be there, too, along with your brothers. You won't be lacking support. And I've known a lot of these people for most of my life. They're good men and, because of the responsibility they've been charged with, they've got to do due diligence."

"I know," she said softly, desultorily taking a bite of the dill pickle spear that had come with her Bobby Darren—also known as a tuna melt. What the sandwich had to do with the singer, she didn't know. "But that doesn't change the fact that having this hearing in the first place is wrong. Ash did nothing wrong. I did nothing wrong."

"Sometimes that's not what makes the difference. I would think that, of anyone, Ash would tell you that."

She slanted a glance of warning at him. "Dad, please. Please don't go off on Ash right now and how doing time for drug-dealing and assault, regardless of how it happened, will always be a strike against him—no matter what he's done or hasn't done since then. I honestly can't take it.''

''I wasn't about to say any such thing,'' Stratton said. He pushed away his own half-eaten Richie Valen, a beef burrito and refried beans. ''I only meant that unfortunate things can happen not by intent but by using bad judgment.''

''And you think I used bad judgment, associating with the so-called bad seed of Rumor.''

''Was it the best judgment, considering what's at stake now?'' her father countered, not ungently.

She remained silent. How to explain it to her father—to anyone? No, it wasn't good judgment, she thought. Because judgment had nothing to do with it. It was love. She had fallen in love with Ash Mc-Donough, and it wouldn't have mattered who he was.

She wanted to go back in time to last night, to their encounter in the garden, and tell Ash that while yes, DeeDee and her children would always bear the stigma of being family to a convicted murderer, that did not wholly define them. It was how someone lived his life after such an awful event that marked the true measure of a person. He may have been guilty of assaulting Dave Reingard—and that was wrong—but since then Ash had never deliberately hurt anyone, and in fact had done his best to help through fighting forest fires....

''Well, if it isn't sweet little Maura Kingsley.''

Maura glanced up, startled. Before her stood Ash himself.

''Ash!'' She'd left a message for him at the Holmes

Ranch this morning, hoping to get the chance to talk to him before he got wind of the rumors flying around. "Oh, I'm so glad you're here."

In fact, her spirits were buoyed immeasurably by the sight of him in his work clothes, looking as ruggedly handsome as he ever had.

Yet he also looked as ruggedly dangerous as the bad seed everyone made him out to be. His gray eyes fairly glowed like the still-treacherous embers of a fire. And they were fixed on her.

"Hello there, powder puff." With his eyes still hot upon her, he greeted her father. "Hey, Stratton. Mind if I have a seat?"

He didn't wait for permission but handily grabbed a nearby chair, set it right beside her and straddled it, negligently crossing his forearms across its back.

"How's the food today?" he asked, boldly reaching out and snagging a few of her French fries. He ate them slowly, sensually, provokingly.

"I-it's…fine," Maura managed to croak, her mouth having gone completely dry.

"You mean you didn't accidentally get served the Frankie Avalon when you'd ordered the Annette Funicello?" He helped himself to another fry—this one from off of Stratton's plate. "Or worse, getting a mixture of both, sort of a Beach Blanket Bass-ackwards?"

He chuckled at his joke, then sobered abruptly.

"Speaking of squeaky-clean, aw-shucks images, powder puff, I hear yours took a beating after last night's kiss between us in your garden. I can't say as I'm all broke up about it. If people only knew the *real* story."

Maura stared at him in concern. He was all bold insolence. She'd never seen him like this before. Never. It was as if a whole different Ash McDonough sat beside her. The Ash McDonough the town believed him to be.

And suddenly she knew what was going on: he'd heard about the trouble with her project, and he was set on showing people he was the one to blame, and that she'd been an unwilling party. That had to be it.

"Ash, you don't have to do this. Really," Maura said in a low voice. She shot her father a significant look, hoping he'd pick up on its meaning.

But Stratton's direct gaze had homed in on Ash. *Oh, no.* She'd seen him that way before, many times—usually when someone displeased him mightily or defied him rashly. The outcome was always grim.

"I know what you're doing, Ash," she said, as calmly and discreetly as she could. It was difficult, for the restaurant was devoid of its normal din of chatter and the clang of silverware. Every person in the place had stopped eating in order to catch the show. She hardly needed eyes in the back of her head to know that every head in the diner was cocked toward their booth. Ash couldn't have picked a better place to cause a scene.

"Please, Ash," Maura said urgently. "You don't have to prove anything—"

"*Really.*" Ash interrupted her with cutting clarity. "I thought that was what it'd always been about with you—proving myself. Provin' I was good enough to even associate with a Kingsley."

He leaned forward confidentially but lowered his

voice not a whit. "Of course, 'associating' wasn't what I was after with you from the start." Silver eyes made a thoroughly brazen perusal of her. "I have to admit, I tried my hardest to get you to give in to me. Even went so far as to push dirt around in that garden of yours to impress you. But I could've dug a hole to China and it wouldn't have mattered with you, would it, Maura?"

"Ash, stop," Maura begged. "Don't do this to yourself."

But he went on with what seemed to her like reckless abandon. "You got the right of it there. I'm done with acting all holier-than-thou to get you to look at me."

He leaned even closer, his face inches from hers and frightening in its intense expression. "I'm not used to striking out with a woman. I'll say it myself. But you were too good for me, isn't that right?" He practically sneered. "Stratton Kingsley's little girl. The do-gooder with a heart of gold—and a shell of cold, cold steel."

His words virtually echoed through the restaurant. Maura couldn't help it. Even though she knew he was putting the attitude on, she gasped in shock and hurt. She had never been spoken to that way in her life. Never.

"Rein it in, McDonough," Stratton growled. "I'll allow you might have a right to feel mistreated by this town, but that gives you no call to take it out on my daughter. Besides, it's not going to help."

Ash didn't blink an eye. "Oh, but I think it does help. A lot. There's about a million things I've been wanting to get off my chest since I came back to Rumor. I'm just startin' with Maura here, letting her know she doesn't have to worry that pretty red head of hers anymore over me tarnishing her precious reputation. I'm done with her.''

Even as biting as his words and tone and meaning were, Maura knew she couldn't let them find their mark in her heart. ''Ash, don't. *I know what you're trying to do.* It won't work. You can't reject me.''

But she had never seen him this way. He looked straight into her eyes, and his were cold hard, steel-gray. If he was bluffing, it was incredibly effective.

Maura searched his gaze desperately, trying to find some shred of the Ash she knew. It wasn't there. And she didn't have the option in this setting of reaching out to him as she had always been able to before, breaking through his defenses, making contact with him through the intimacy that neither of them had ever been able to resist.

She laid her hand on his, curling her fingers around it, trying in any case to twine between them some thread of that connection. ''I don't believe you. You can't mean any of this.''

He stared at her hand for a long moment, then lifted his gaze to hers. It was as distant as she'd ever seen a person look in her life.

And it roused in her a fear she hadn't even known she'd harbored. A fear that she *didn't* know him or what he was capable of.

''I don't believe you,'' she once more protested. But her voice lacked the conviction of before.

''Well, believe it, powder puff,'' he drawled. ''I

don't need this bull crap. I can sure enough find a whole lot more friendly women down the road."

He stood and pivoted the chair behind him so that he practically hovered over her. His gaze bored into hers. "And as soon as I pack my bags and draw my last paycheck, that's where I'm headin'."

Maura's heart stopped and started ten times in the ensuing half minute before she found her voice.

"You...you're leaving Rumor?" Maura asked, stunned, numb.

"That's right."

It was the one action he could take that she couldn't defend against. How could she convince Ash that their love was strong enough to survive this ordeal if he wasn't around to convince?

She needed time—time alone with him to get past this hardened stranger who sat before her and reach the Ash she knew and loved. And who loved her.

She made one last try. "Ash...what about what we shared together?"

His lashes flickered before he came right back at her with that indifferent gaze. If anything, it was even more lifeless. He took her chin between his thumb and forefinger.

"Who's the gullible one now?" he murmured.

Then he let her go and was gone.

The restaurant was deathly quiet. Misty, the teenage waitress, cracked her gum by accident and promptly burst into tears.

Maura found her father's gaze on her yet again, and it was only by keeping eye contact with him that she was able to prevent herself from following Misty's lead.

Yet Maura lifted her chin. No, she wouldn't cry, she vowed stubbornly. She was a Kingsley. Such outpourings of emotion were done in the privacy of her home.

But it occurred to Maura that her home was no longer the girlish bedroom at the family ranch where she was surrounded by the comfort and support of those who loved her best.

No, home was the little apartment down the street that, in a rite of passage, she'd moved into barely two weeks ago with excitement and high hopes for her future as an independent woman of the world.

Well, now she'd just endured another rite, and it was too bad Ash wasn't around to see it. No longer could he claim that she'd never had anything truly awful happen to her.

For watching Ash McDonough walk out of her life had broken her heart into a thousand pieces.

Chapter Ten

The evening sun in his eyes, Ash drove past the sign that said Entering Rumor City Limits for what he had to believe would be the last time in his life.

He should have been on cloud nine at leaving this place and its memories forever. As it was, his spirits were lower than river silt.

He had no choice but to leave. Still, he couldn't help feeling he was letting everyone down, himself most of all.

After returning to the Holmes Ranch and working the rest of the afternoon, he'd tracked down Colby at HQ and let his boss know it was his last day.

Understandably, Colby had been surprised.

"You can't mean it, Ash," he'd said, removing worn leather gloves that looked as if they'd been around since Colby's rodeo days. He stuffed them in his back pocket. "If it's money, I'll double your wages right now. Triple 'em."

Ash had actually smiled. "You know it's not money—although I'm tempted to hang around so you have to make good on that offer." He shook his head. "No, it's just…time. I saw Emmy the other night, and we had a long talk. It helped us both, a lot. It also helped to see that she's doing real well. She's happy in Big Timber. And happy to be close to Rumor and friends here, without being in the thick of it."

He'd given his own leather gloves a thoroughly unnecessary going over. "Now that we're on the road to reconciling, it won't matter whether I'm there, either."

In the edge of his vision he saw Colby shift on his feet.

"Well, it's your business and no other's what you do," Colby had finally said. He hesitated, then went on. "I can't know what you've been through these past ten years, Ash. No one can but you. But I think I pretty much imagine it to've been one rough road. So for what it's worth, you've got my support."

Chin still tucked, Ash had nodded. "That means a lot to me, Colby."

His boss had slapped him on the back. "That doesn't mean I'm quite ready to accept your resignation. Take the night to sleep on it, will you? I'll call you in the morning, and if you're still set on leaving, I'll have your paycheck ready for you."

Ash had said he'd do that, but he knew in his heart he wouldn't change his mind. And he couldn't change his heart.

He'd always put serving those five years in prison

at the top of his list of Things I Don't Need to Repeat in Life. After today, another had taken top billing— leaving Maura.

He couldn't think about her right now. He was still too close to doing what she'd suggested last night and running away with her to anywhere but here.

But Ash did have one last task to take care of before he went back to his apartment and packed. Luckily or unluckily—it depended upon how one looked at it— everything he owned could fit into his pickup.

He drove through town, heading to the north side where the cemetery was located.

But as Ash turned the corner at Lost Lane, a smell in the air coming in his open window made the hair on back of his neck stand up straight.

Madly, he glanced around, searching the sky above the housetops. Then he saw it: smoke. And it was coming from the Reingard place.

Ash gunned his pickup, was halfway out of the driver's door before he'd shoved it into park in front of DeeDee's home. Just as he did, she saw him from where she was hovering on the east side of the house and came tearing toward him, eyes wide and frantic.

"Oh, Ash! My house is on fire!"

He caught her by the shoulders. "What happened?"

"I was pressing…some fall leaves…between waxed paper to take to my daycare…children when the phone rang." Her words and breathing came in panicky gasps. "I must have set the iron…too close to the pa-per…because when I came back into the kitchen ten minutes later…it seemed like the whole room was ablaze!"

Ash peered at the side of the house where the smoke was coming from. It was hard to tell, but the fire didn't look uncontainable—yet. "You call the fire department?"

"Just a minute ago, but you know how half the squad is still fighting the forest fire! Who knows how long it'll take for them to get here and how many will come."

"They'll get here, don't worry," he assured her.

"But that's the thing! It might be too late!" She clutched his shirtfront. "Ash, Parker's in there! He went back in before I could stop him!"

Ash's blood froze. "He is?"

"I made some stupid comment about all of the memories our family would lose if the fire department didn't arrive in time to save the house! I think Parker went in to save some of the photo albums."

She pressed her fisted hands to her temples. "If I lose my boy over that careless comment, I don't know what I'll do. Heavens, Ash, half of those memories with Dave are almost too painful to keep! I've been shouting up to my bedroom window, but there's no sign of him." Fear ravaged her features. Tears filled her eyes and spilled over. "I can't lose my baby, Ash! I can't."

"You won't." He caught her close to him briefly in a reassuring embrace. "I'll get him out."

Releasing her, Ash ran for his truck. He had some of his fire gear there, but it would be meager help in this case. Even if he'd been outfitted in fully protective firefighting gear, it wasn't the flames that were the real danger in a house fire. Inside the house, smoke would be fast accumulating. It would suffocate Parker.

Jerking open the cab door, Ash pulled out his fire pack and dumped it wholesale on the ground. He rummaged through Nomex shirt and pants and lug-soled boots for the essentials: his helmet, goggles, face mask and Pulaski.

He donned the helmet and goggles and Velcroed the mask around his neck as he ran back to the burning house, his mind already calculating the best entry route. And praying the fire department would get here soon. The vegetation around the house and into the hills was so dangerously dry it would take only one floating ember to start another out-of-control forest fire…just like the one he'd been caught in with Maura—

"Ash!"

He whipped around to find the object of his thoughts sprinting toward him.

Maura was gasping and she came up short in front of him. "I'd stopped in to visit Val Fairchild and saw the smoke. Oh, poor DeeDee!"

"Yes." He started for the house again, not even thinking of shortening his stride as she tried to keep up.

"You're going in?" she asked, eyeing the Pulaski in his hand as she ran beside him. "Why? Hasn't someone called 911?"

"Parker's in there," he said tersely, the stiff fabric of the mask around his neck scratching his chin. "And there's no sign of the fire department as of this moment. Someone's gotta go inside to get him."

He didn't want her here for a whole slew of reasons, not the least among them that it tore him into tiny pieces just to see her, but mainly because he knew what would happen next.

Maura didn't disappoint. "I'm going in with you," she announced.

He ignored her as he came up on DeeDee, who'd gone back to shouting at an upstairs window.

"Which door did he go in?" he asked.

"The front—but I think he went upstairs to my bedroom, toward the back of the house." She pointed. "That's the window up there."

And the fire started in the kitchen, which was directly below the bedroom, on the main floor.

There was no sound of sirens blaring, only the crackle of the fire, which was growing by the second.

"All right, then," Ash said grimly. "I'm going in. Let whoever's in charge know when the fire department gets here there're two people inside and where we're located."

"Make that three," Maura said from behind him.

Ash turned on her in a fury. "Don't even think about it!"

She stood up to him, not batting an eye. "I've got firefighting experience. I can help."

He grabbed her shoulders none too gently. "Don't fight me on this, Maura. I don't have time."

Her eyes flashed up at him like two blue flares. "If this is about me being a powder puff that can't handle the job, you can just stuff that attitude, cowboy."

"It's not that!" He gave a huff of frustration. He needed to get inside that house. "Maura, for once in your life stop bein' so damned stubborn and listen to reason. You can't go in there. It's dangerous enough that I'm goin' in there with so little protection. We don't need something happening to both of us. I wouldn't be able to live with myself if it did.''

''But things *do* happen to people, Ash—to ourselves and to the people we love—whether we mean to or not, and even with the best of intentions. We *have* to learn to live with what happens and with ourselves.''

Sadness etched her gaze—sadness for him. ''And Ash, you can't start truly living with yourself today until you learn to live with who you were yesterday.''

He stared down at her, not sure what she meant, as he hadn't been quite sure what her mother had meant when Carolyn had offered advice about going after what he wanted one hundred percent. But then, he had a feeling that such a uniquely Kingsleyesque outlook would always elude him. They simply couldn't know what it was like for those unlike themselves.

''I've gotta get to Parker,'' he muttered, pulling his mask into place. ''Stay with DeeDee, Maura. She needs you.''

For once she didn't protest, and he was thankful for that, although she continued to look at him in that way that truly made him feel like a failure. Not that she thought him one, but that by not reaching out in faith and hope as she did, he failed himself more than anyone else.

He couldn't think about it now. There was one thing he could do, one way he couldn't fail.

Ash took the front steps two at a time and barreled through the front door. Smoke was everywhere. Unfortunately, his mask wasn't a full-fledged gas mask; it would limit the amount of smoke he might inhale, but not as well as a more comprehensive respiratory mask.

He started up the staircase, shouting Parker's name. There was no response.

Ash didn't hesitate when he reached the top of the stairs but ran down the hallway. The last door on the left was closed, and when he grasped its knob the door stopped about six inches open. Through the haze of smoke he saw what looked like the back of a cabinet or armoire that had fallen across the doorway. Strewn across the wood floor were dozens of photos that had apparently spilled from the cardboard shoebox tipped on its side.

Peering hard, Ash made out something else, and it made his blood run cold: a forearm and hand sticking out from under the wardrobe. Somehow it must have fallen on the teenager, knocking him out and pinning him beneath it.

Putting his shoulder against the door, Ash tried shifting the armoire just enough to widen the opening a few inches without causing the heavy piece of furniture to move significantly and perhaps doing more damage to Parker. It didn't budge.

After wasting a few precious seconds in which he tried levering the handle of the Pulaski against the door and the jamb, Ash had still only gotten the door open barely another inch. Not near wide enough for his frame to squeeze through.

Then a masculine voice behind him said, "Try it now."

Ash pivoted, reflexively raising the Pulaski in defense. The fine hairs on his neck stood up when he encountered nothing but the haze-filled hallway behind him. "What the hell?"

"Just do it!" the voice said again, and if it hadn't been for the fact that his adrenaline was already running at an all-time high, Ash would have jumped out of his skin.

That was when it hit him.

"Guy Cantrell?" he said, feeling incredulous and ridiculous at the same time. "You mean for once the rumors are right and you *are* invisible?"

"Look. Do you want some help or not?" the disembodied voice said with thin patience. "This town's already lost three people to fire in the past few months. Let's not make it five!"

It was on Ash's lips to point out that Guy still stood accused not only of killing two of those people but also being behind the mysterious disappearance of Old Man Jackson. If there was one thing Ash's experience had ingrained in him, however, it was not to judge as quickly and harshly as he himself had been judged.

"You're right," Ash said to the nothingness in front of him. He'd have felt pretty foolish except he had no time to. He turned around again, pressing his shoulder to the door. "On three. One…two…three!"

This time when Ash shoved, he could feel the extra leverage that came from having two men straining with all their might to shift the armoire. At first it moved only a scant millimeter, then it gave a little more, then a little more. Ash gave a great grunt that was echoed in his ear—and suddenly the opening was a foot wide.

"Let's go," Ash panted, squeezing sideways between the door and its jamb. Once inside the room he removed his helmet and mask and bent to check on DeeDee's son.

"Parker!" The boy lay face up beneath the armoire, not stirring. His eyes were closed and his face pale, but when Ash felt the young man's wrist for a pulse, it was sure and strong.

"Help me get this thing off him," he said, assuming Guy had been able to follow him into the room.

Ash grasped the top edge of the armoire on one side and again counted off. "One, two, three, heave!"

Up came the massive seven-foot-tall armoire, which teetered dangerously for a moment before Ash and his invisible companion gave a mighty push that sent it banging back against the wall. Instantly he was at Parker's side again, assessing his condition.

"Is he okay?" the voice asked above Ash.

"It looks like he has a concussion at the very least, maybe some cracked ribs. Parker!" He shook the young man lightly. "Wake up, kid!"

Parker groaned, then coughed. His eyelids fluttered briefly before opening. The expression in his eyes as he stared up at Ash was cloudy but comprehending. "Ash? What happened?"

"You must've been reaching for the photos stacked on top of the armoire and pulled it down on top of you."

"Oh, yeah." The boy coughed again. Opening the door had allowed much more smoke into the room.

"Where the hell is the fire department?" Ash muttered. Maybe there was still time for him, Guy and the boy to make it down the front stairs and outside.

Ash fitted his mask over Parker's nose and mouth. "C'mon, kid. We've gotta get out of here. Think you can walk?"

"I dunno." Ash helped him sit up, but when Parker tried to stand, he buckled at the waist almost instantly and slumped back onto the floor, wincing and grabbing his leg.

"It's my kneecap. I hope it's not busted," he gasped. "But...I'll walk on it, since my life depends on it."

He gazed up at Ash, who knew that if Parker did put pressure on that leg, there was a good chance he'd worsen the injury to his knee, perhaps irreparably. And if so, Ash thought with a pang of sympathy, there went the rest of Parker's senior year in football and the chance for a much-needed scholarship.

Crouching with his arm about Parker's shoulders, Ash wondered madly what to do. Guy had closed the door behind them, keeping more smoke from seeping into the room. The hallway and staircase would soon be impassable, though, if they weren't already.

And with the fire directly below them, they all had little time left if they were to escape alive.

Only then did Ash hear the distant wail of a siren.

Hugging herself, Maura stared at the frame house, black smoke flowing from the edges of nearly every window. Except the one DeeDee had pointed to as being where her son might be.

One could only pray that it meant Ash was there

with Parker and had closed off the room—and perhaps waited now for rescue, rather than risk leaving the house and being overcome by the deadly smoke.

But was that the best course to take at this point? Maura wondered. It might be the most cautious, but trying to outsmart a fire was a dangerous game, fraught with hazards at every turn. She knew. Oh, she knew all too well.

Her heart steadied for a scant beat or two as around the corner came the Rumor fire engine. It careered to a stop as men in fire gear leaped to the ground.

To her surprise, her brother Reed was among them. It could only mean one thing: the Rumor forest fire was finally contained, and Reed was home for good.

DeeDee ran to him. "My son! And Ash McDonough! They're in there! Upstairs in the back far-right bedroom, I think!"

"We'll get 'em out, DeeDee." Reed issued staccato orders to his men. "Smitty, you're on hydrant. Blackburn, get a ladder up to the second-floor window there on the east side of the house. West, Peterson, take the front door. Get a hose on that flame coming out the window below it, Franz. Move! There're people in there."

"What took you so long to get here?" Maura asked him when he'd finished shouting out assignments.

"Hello to you, too, sis," Reed said, smiling in that devil-may-care way she'd missed. "The call for the fire came in while the squad was out checking a report on a trash fire south of town. The good news is, we're fully manned again."

He sobered as he surveyed the scene. Despite the

cheeky smile he'd treated her to, Maura could tell from the two lines drawn on either side of her brother's mouth that the long hours spent on the Rumor forest fire had taken their toll. Thank goodness the fire had finally been contained. It seemed as if it had gone on forever.

But now there was the risk of this one burning out of control and starting the cycle all over again.

"So Ash McDonough went in after the kid?" Reed asked Maura. His gaze never left his men as they swarmed around the burning house.

She, too, focused on the upper-floor window where Ash and Parker were. "Yes. I wanted to go in, too, but he said he'd hog-tie me or something to the equivalent."

Another smile touched the corner of Reed's mouth. "You mean there's a man in this town who's learned how to handle my stubborn little sister?"

Had she not been so worried about Ash and Parker, Maura would never have bristled at her brother's teasing comment. "I wouldn't call myself hard to handle *or* stubborn!"

"You're the youngest and the only girl in the Kingsley brood," he said tolerantly. "Face it, sis. You had to develop some grit if you wanted to survive. And you had one of the best role models for that."

"Dad?" she asked.

"No...Mom." He captured her shoulders in a hug. "Don't get me wrong. I'm not sayin' that your brand of determination is bad. It can sure cause some hair-raising moments for those who love you. But it's always amazing how you make things come out right. You never stop going for it.''

Within the security of her older brother's embrace, Maura continued to fix her gaze on the burning house as she pondered his words. She wondered what he'd say once he learned how she'd failed with Ash—failed because she had never failed before. It seemed impossible to her that that paradox could exist, could keep them apart. Could cause her to lose him.

Was there truly nothing she could do but let him leave the way he felt he had to?

"Mom told me about your hearing with the development group when I stopped by before driving into town. Isn't it about time for it to start?" Reed asked.

She frowned at her watch. "In about ten minutes."

He released her to give quick instructions to one of his men before turning back to her. "Well, I'll be a little late and looking somewhat worse for wear, but I'll be there for support as soon as we get Parker and Ash out and get the fire under control. It's too important to miss, you know, even with these kinds of circumstances."

The phrase struck a chord. *Too important to miss, no matter the circumstances. You ought to know that.* It was what Dave Reingard had told Ash.

"Actually, I'm not leaving till I know Ash and Parker are safe," Maura said thoughtfully.

Reed pulled his gaze away from the fire only long enough to peer at her in concern. "Maura, I don't think this is something you want to be even a little late to. From what Mom said, the group's already questioning your dependability. Why tempt fate?"

She crossed her arms. "Maybe the question is, Why not tempt it?"

Reed just shook his head as he left her side to confer with one of his men. Maura knew what he was thinking: that she was still the stubborn little sister he'd grown up with.

And perhaps she was. Because she'd just gotten her wind back...and her hope, that somehow—with love and persistence—she and Ash could still make it come out right for both of them.

The smoke was pervasive, a living thing. It became hard to see, hard to breathe, hard to think.

Ash reviewed their options: likely, the firemen would investigate rescue through the interior of the house first, even while putting a ladder at the window. But who knew how long it would be before they got to this room.

"We can probably still get you out the front door," Ash told Parker, "if we're supporting you on either side."

Parker glanced around in bewilderment. "Who else is here?"

Ash had his mouth open to answer when a hand clamped down on his shoulder. "No one else can know I'm here and invisible," Guy whispered into Ash's ear.

Ash wanted to ask why but again wasn't about to be the one to judge the man. However, blowing Guy's cover might be unavoidable.

"I meant that I could get you out, Parker," Ash said, trying to limit the number of breaths he took. "But we have to make a decision soon—"

The window shattered, startling them. An arm pushed aside the sheers. The hazy form of a helmet hovered in the opening, looking specter-like.

"Parker! Ash! Are you in here?"

"Ye—" Ash coughed. "Yes, we're here!" He vaulted over the bed and tore the sheers and drapes from their rods, getting them out of the way as glass crunched under the soles of his boots. He recognized the fireman as Ray Scoggins, the rural route deliverer for the Rumor Post Office.

"The boy's suffered a concussion and probably a broken kneecap but he's alert," Ash reported. He peered past Ray's shoulder. The ground was twenty feet below. It'd be quite a climb down to it with Parker's injuries. "I don't know if the best way out is taking him down this ladder."

"We don't have much other choice," Ray said. "The smoke is too thick in the hallway. There's a good chance it'd overcome anyone going out that way."

With the opening of the window creating a draft, black smoke was seeping in around every edge of the door, Ash noticed.

He nodded grimly. "All right. I'll help him over to the window. Do you want me to carry him down? He's one strapping football player, I'll kid you not."

The fireman actually cracked a smile. "I can manage, if that's all I've got to carry. You can come down behind him."

"Sure enough."

There was the voice in Ash's ear again, making him jump. "Wait! How'll I get out?"

Damn. He'd forgotten all about Guy.

"Look, Ray, why don't you climb down and dump your ax while I get Parker over to the window."

Waiting only an instant after the fireman complied, Ash stooped under pretense of gathering the drapes to stuff into the crack under the door as he whispered, "Come down the ladder after me, Guy. I'll make sure to leave enough time once I'm on the ground for you to clear the bottom of the ladder."

"All right," Guy whispered back, "just don't let anyone see me—"

The voice broke off as Ash heard a gasp of pain— then watched as flashes of what looked like lungs and liver and intestines shimmered in front of his eyes.

Utter horror shot through him like a dynamite blast. Another gasp behind him made him turn, and Ash saw Parker staring at the same gruesome sight.

"Wh-what's that?" the young man stuttered, obviously as stunned as Ash, especially when there was another tortured gasp. This time he saw a skull, half-covered with skin and hair, the other half muscle and tendons shaped into a grimace of sheer agony.

Ash hadn't time to explain. "Guy! Guy, what's happening? Are you all right?"

He automatically reached toward the quaking image. His fingers closed around not viscera but what felt like a very real, very normal arm. He clamped his other hand around Guy's other arm. "Guy, what's wrong?"

"It's...it's the formula...for my burn ointment." The flesh beneath Ash's palms shuddered as if an electric current were going through it. It made his own skin crawl. "It's wearing off s-somehow, and it feels like it's going to k-k-kill me when it does."

"We've got to get you help!" Ash said.

"No! N-not yet. Not till I've got a plan."

Ash could only stand there helplessly as Guy suffered through another attack that was like something out of a sci-fi movie.

Then it seemed to be over. Invisible again, Guy went limp in Ash's hands, and he eased the science teacher to the floor and wrapped the bedspread around his shoulders. Or what Ash thought were Guy's shoulders.

"That was the worst yet," Guy said on a pant. "Usually once the episodes pass, I'll remain invisible for some time. But Ash...I don't think I can walk out of here under my own power."

There was a pause. "You two go—you and Parker. Save yourselves."

"Leaving you is not an option," Ash said. "So let's not waste time arguing about it and instead make a plan to get everyone safely out of here."

He strode to the bathroom located in the bedroom and flicked on the light. Plenty of towels that could be soaked and used for protection from the heat and smoke. He threw half a dozen into the bathtub and turned on the faucet to do just that.

Coming back into the bedroom, Ash went to crouch at Parker's side. "Here, loop your arm around my neck so I can help you over to the window. You're going to cause a distraction once you're on the ground so that I can get Guy out."

"Ash, they say he killed his wife," the teenager whispered through the fire mask, casting a nervous glance toward the hunched figure in the bedspread. "And that Templeton guy."

"In this town, what people say and what's actually the truth are, a lot of the time, worlds apart, kid," Ash said grimly.

Parker looked at him skeptically. "Like what they're sayin' about you and Maura Kingsley?"

Ash studied him a moment. "You've worked with Michael Cantrell, Guy's nephew, in the garden. What's he said to you about the situation?"

"That his uncle's innocent," was Parker's dubious answer.

"Then trust him," Ash said. "Trust me, 'cause I'm telling you that I'm not the bad seed people are making me out to be. I'd never hurt Maura, not for the world."

"Ash! Ash, I'm back for the boy."

It was Ray. Ash and Parker stared at each other for a long moment. Then, even though the boy was in obvious pain, perspiration beading on his forehead, he nodded firmly. "I'll make it happen."

"Got him right here," Ash said. Counting to three, he hefted the teenager to his feet, making sure to support his injured side.

The two hop-stepped over to the window, which Ray had raised from the outside to create a larger opening for Parker to go through.

Parker perched gingerly on the sill, wincing as Ash and Ray maneuvered his legs through the window so that he was facing the fireman.

"Now, I'm gonna have you lean toward me and just fold yourself over my left shoulder," Ray instructed him. "Try to stay as loose and relaxed as you can, like an ol' rag doll, and I'll do the rest. Ash, wait till we're on the ground, then come on down."

Ash said nothing. Parker did as he was instructed. Ray grunted once as he took on the boy's weight, then started to descend the ladder.

Ash turned back into the room. The bedspread lay in a heap on the wood floor. He glanced around, wondering why he did so. Even if Guy had been fully visible and dressed in a neon-orange hunting vest, Ash would have had difficulty seeing him. The smoke was thick as pea soup. It seared his windpipe with every breath he took.

Then he peered into the bathroom and saw Guy had soaked what had to be DeeDee's navy blue terry robe and donned it. He'd also wrapped one of the wet towels around his face so it showed the disembodied outline of his nose, mouth and chin.

"The damp material feels good on my skin, for some reason," he said.

"And it'll protect you from the heat," Ash said. He grabbed a towel for himself and wrapped it around the lower half of his face, bandit-style. "So here's the plan. I'll carry you piggy-back style with the bedspread wrapped around both of us. Hopefully it'll look like it's just me underneath, but the distraction Parker will cause will help ensure no one gets that good a look."

He plucked the bedspread from the floor as he continued talking. "I noticed a hedge of bushes about twenty feet from the house. When I clear the front door, I'll make straight for the hedge and let the bedspread, with you in it, slide off my back. Once you're there you can get your bearings and hopefully make your way out when you're feeling better. At least you'll be hidden if you get one of your attacks again."

He hesitated, clutching the bedspread in both hands. "Look, Guy, I'm probably the least likely person to stick my nose in someone else's business, but I strongly urge you to come clean about what happened with your wife and Templeton as soon as you can."

"Will people understand, though?" Guy's muffled voice was apprehensive. "They think I *murdered* them. I'd never do something like that. Never."

"And those who know you and care about you believe that you didn't do it, even without an explanation," Ash told him with complete truthfulness. "They'll stand behind you, no matter what."

He motioned Guy over to the window. "Now, get a good lungful of air, then let's roll."

By some miracle, Ash's plan came off without a hitch.

The smoke in the hallway obliterated all light, and Ash had to go by feel, his eyes stinging even behind his goggles, his lungs nearly bursting from holding his breath to keep from inhaling the tissue-scorching smoke and from the effort of carrying a 170-pound load.

But he made it, he and Guy.

Simply by dint of coming down the ladder on Ray's shoulder put Parker at center stage. That and his mother rushing to him with cries of relief. The crowd that had gathered shifted to watch the joyful scene and, because everyone expected Ash to be the next one down, he found he had a clear shot to the hedge in the opposite direction.

There, he deposited Guy without incident. The science teacher huddled under one bush and assured Ash he would be fine, to go and alert the firemen that he was out of the burning house, so they wouldn't try to go back up the ladder when Ash didn't appear at the window.

Seeing the wisdom in the suggestion, Ash did exactly that, and was astounded to find himself hailed a hero—at least by DeeDee, who hugged him so hard around the middle he thought his lungs *would* burst.

"Oh, Ash, thank you, thank you!" she exclaimed. She apparently found nothing strange about him appearing from around the side of the house, although Ash noticed a few of the firemen exchanging puzzled glances.

He didn't see Maura, and realized that it was after seven-thirty. She would be at her hearing right now.

"Parker says you lifted that huge old wardrobe of mine off him," DeeDee said, interrupting his thoughts. "I don't know how you did it, because it weighs a ton, but I'm so thankful you could."

"You're more than welcome, DeeDee," Ash said hoarsely, his throat raw from the smoke he'd inhaled.

Parker had been carried to the ambulance that must have arrived when Ash was in the house, and he could see that the boy had been put on oxygen and was being checked over by Jim Brenner, the pediatrician who must have come over from the Rumor Family Clinic.

Waving off medical attention for himself, Ash returned his gaze to DeeDee's house. He noticed that she, too, stood staring at the structure, which, though Rumor's finest had been able to contain the fire, looked to be severely damaged.

"I'm sorry, DeeDee," he murmured. "I hope your insurance company won't declare it a total loss, that something can be saved."

Her gaze still on the blackened house, she said, "There is no insurance. I let the coverage lapse a few months ago so that I could pay other bills that'd come up. I'd planned on starting coverage up again next month."

"Ah, DeeDee," Ash said. "It must seem like you can't catch a break for love or money."

A tear slid down her cheek, which she swiped at impatiently. "It does. But I refuse to let this setback get me down. How can I, when my precious son came out of it safe? And so what if he doesn't get that football scholarship that he'd been counting on? We'll get him into college, one way or another. Our family will survive."

He had to admire her gumption, her optimism after all that she and her family had gone through. He didn't doubt a bit that the Reingards would go on—just as his own family would have done ten years ago despite the troubles they'd endured. He hadn't had to quit high school.

Yet he had, just as he'd gotten caught up in the Brannigans' schemes. He couldn't change the past—so he needed to let go of it.

"DeeDee," Ash said abruptly.

She raised her eyebrows at him in inquiry. "Yes, Ash?"

"You probably don't remember, but ten years ago, when Dave was a deputy with the sheriff's department, he was sent to come get me at my mother's for missing the hearing for my trial. And I assaulted him. I'm pretty sure he couldn't have hidden the broken nose I gave him," he cracked wryly, then sobered. "I just wanted you to know—I was the one who did it."

She smiled. "I knew it was you, Ash."

"Really? But you didn't seem to know me when we first met in the garden."

"I didn't remember then. It was only later, when I got to thinking about it."

Ash concentrated on the firemen, who continued to spray down the smoldering fire in the dying evening light. "Do you know, then, what happened at my mother's house that day?"

"Not the whole story, by any means." She set her hand on his forearm, and he looked at her. "Dave had seemed pretty disturbed, and I asked him why. He just said he'd had one of those days that happen sometimes in law enforcement. He would only say that it had involved you and your family."

"Then I have him to thank for keeping it to himself. It was...decent of him."

"Yes, Dave isn't a completely unredeemable man."

Ash glanced at her sharply. "Funny you should use that word—redeemable." He swallowed hard. "That afternoon has haunted me ever since. It's the real reason, more than the drug conviction, that I felt I had to come back to Rumor and clear my name, for the sake of those who cared for me."

"And am I ever glad you had that purpose, Ash," DeeDee said.

"Really? I can't see as how I've been able to fulfill it."

"Oh, but you have, even if it wasn't how you'd thought it would happen! Just think, if you hadn't felt you had to come back here to make things right, you wouldn't have been here to save Parker. You saved Maura from the forest fire, too, didn't you?"

She gave his arm a shake. "Be grateful for *that*, Ash. We don't always get such clear-cut signs as to what our purpose is on earth—or the meaning in the suffering we endure. It's like with Dave—how can I regret having married him even knowing now the heartache that came out of it? He's the father of my five beautiful children."

Ash stared at her. He had never thought of it that way. Instead, he had always dwelt on the pain and hurt he had caused—to his mother, Emmy and now Maura. He still couldn't ascribe to DeeDee's view that there was a reason for such pain.

But that redemption might be found in the ashes of such devastation…well, that was a philosophy he just might be able to get behind.

Something made him turn at that moment, and across the yard filled with people Ash's gaze collided with Maura's. *She's still here?* he thought. Her hearing must have started fifteen minutes ago. She couldn't miss it!

Yet…she *was* still here, even at the risk of her future. She'd do that for him. And God, the love he saw in those blue eyes even now, even after how he'd hurt her today! It was unbelievable, almost unendurable. He did not deserve it.

He couldn't give in to it. He had to do the right

thing before the wrong thing occurred. He had to be strong, for Maura's sake.

And so Ash turned away again. Walked away again. But he knew that regardless of the rightness of his actions, he was damned to serve the rest of his life in a prison of his own making.

Chapter Eleven

Maura pushed open the main door to the town library and walked down the hallway to the meeting room in a daze. The past hour and a half waiting for the house fire to be contained and everyone to get out safely had been nerve-racking, to say the least. And then Ash had turned from her, yet again. That had been hard to endure. Terribly hard.

Not that she'd expected him to open his arms to her. It would take time for him to realize the strength of her love for him. Of the rightness of their love for each other.

But that wouldn't happen by her tracking him all the way to the Canadian border and back. Nor was it dependent upon whether he was in Rumor or not. No, it was a place in his heart that he needed to go to before he could come home for good.

Maura stopped just outside the closed door to the meeting room. It still seemed inconceivable to her that inside she might lose the remainder of everything she'd ever cared for.

Taking a deep breath, she entered the room and noted with dismay the number of people who filled the chairs. Apparently, this was simply too good a show to miss. Searching the faces, she was surprised to find her father missing, although her mother and brothers, along with their families, had taken seats at the back of the room.

She wondered if there was something wrong. But then Carolyn smiled at her encouragingly, and the wave of love that radiated from them all nearly took Maura's breath away.

"Glad you could make it, Maura," Willard Alden said from the front of the room. Maura had forgotten that Willard was Alice's son—and the chairperson of the development group. He would, of course, have gotten a veritable earful about how the bad seed of Rumor had stigmatized Maura. She may as well have it tattooed on her forehead: Soiled Goods.

The other members she knew only slightly, as businessmen in town and friends of her father. Surely they'd listen to her and act fairly. But then there was Dodge Baker, the local, self-appointed ombudsman. Every project coming up for the group's approval had to pass his rigorous sniff test. And judging from the perennial scowl on his face, to him, everything smelled bad.

In fact, it was Dodge himself who followed up Willard's comment with a sarcastic "Yeah, at least you didn't bring your boyfriend. That would've been about as reckless as your letting Ash McDonough around those little ones.''

"Well, I'm here now and at the group's disposal," Maura said crisply with all of her mother's regal bearing, not dignifying Dodge's remark with a response. She held her head high as she strode to the front of the room and took her seat behind the small table facing the panel of men, feeling as if she were about to undergo the modern-day, Rumor version of the Salem witch trials.

"Well now," Willard said, clearing his throat. He rustled the few papers before him importantly, obviously loving the spotlight. "I call to order this meeting of the Rumor Development Group. All members present—" he doffed his reading glasses to take an ostensible reckoning of the room's occupants "—except Stratton Kingsley. Which is of little matter since he wouldn't be able to vote tonight. You'd think he'd want to show up for the discussion, though."

Hands clasped on the table in front of her, Maura sat straight and motionless, as if a steel rod held her in place.

Willard went on. "Tonight we have before the members the matter of whether to refuse Maura Kingsley the funding to develop a ranch for disadvantaged children on the twenty-acre parcel of land encompassing the former home of the widow Ernestine Brickart. Everyone has read Maura's proposal and listened to her presentation on the project. There's no doubt that it's a sound plan and a needed service in this area. That's not up for discussion.''

He glanced to either side of him at the other two members of the group, who so far had revealed nothing of their leanings on the matter. "What is up for debate is whether Maura Kingsley is of the moral character and sound judgment to run the program, since she recently has been known to have consorted with Ash McDonough, a convicted felon on parole who was allowed by Maura to volunteer with the children under her care."

Consorting? Maura had the wildest urge to act out, to tell such a pack of exaggerated lies that they'd see how ludicrous this situation was. Why not say she'd been riding shotgun in the truck that Ash had been driving when he got busted for drugs, and he was back to demand his compensation for not squealing on her?

"I actually believe we can take care of this pretty quickly, Willard," Dodge spoke up. He cleared his throat, then did it again, more loudly, when the errant whispering between her mother and Reed, who'd just arrived, didn't immediately cease.

Carolyn smiled benignly at Dodge. "Please do go on, Dodge."

His scowl screwed up a notch. "As I was saying. I have it on good authority that Ash McDonough himself admitted, in public, that he'd tried a bunch of different ways to corrupt Maura, including pretending he liked volunteering at the children's garden. She resisted."

He sat back in his chair, hands spread on his ample stomach. "Now, I'll grant it wasn't the smartest thing to do to let an ex-con anywhere near kids, but then, how could a young thing like Maura know the workings of the criminal mind?"

Dodge gave her a wink, clearly enjoying playing the role of the magnanimous Daddy Warbucks, especially to one of the royal family of Rumor.

"Anyway, I also understand that McDonough has left Rumor for good. Or is that good riddance?" Dodge actually chuckled. "So if Maura here can assure the group she's learned her lesson, I propose we give her the okay on the ranch."

Willard nodded. Maura interpreted his expression as thoughtful. It could just as easily have meant he had gas. "I could see clear to endorsing that," he said. "Although we'll want to do some oversight of the project for the first year or so, just to make sure she stays on the right track. But I've always said people deserve a second chance, and I think Maura deserves one. Roy and Oscar, what do you think?"

Maura had an idea that her face, at that moment, resembled her father's at its most apoplectic. She wasn't about to wait for the other two men to weigh in with their pithy opinions either for or against her.

Slowly she rose, every bit of her five-foot, two-inch height bristling with conviction.

"Everyone deserves a second chance, you say?" she asked. She turned, her gaze skewering each person in the room. "When has this town given Ash Mc-Donough that chance? It's more like the majority of you have never given *yourselves* the chance to get to know him on his own merit. Instead you've chosen to subsist on recycled rumors that you add embellishments to when the gossip gets stale. In fact, I can barely believe I'm having to stand here and defend him after he saved Parker Reingard's life today."

She set her hands on her hips. "Well, shame on you. Shame on you all."

She swung back to the four men at the front of the room. "Let the record show once and for all that Ash McDonough is *not* a bad seed," Maura announced. "Sure, he made a mistake, but he did his time *and* he came back to town—a town that's been, at the very least, unwelcoming—with the intent of making amends and a respectable life for himself."

Maura placed the heels of her hands on the table in front of her and leaned forward passionately. "It was not bad judgment on my part to have Ash volunteer with the children in the garden. Yes, I asked him! Each of those kids, from the older ones like Michael Cantrell on down to the littlest of them, have benefited enormously from Ash's experience and wisdom and understanding. He brings with him a soul-deep awareness of what it's like to be less than perfect, to be bereft of the hope of redeeming himself. To wonder if he can be loved."

Her voice cracked perilously. "So here's the deal *I'm* putting before the members of the Rumor Development Group—that not only am I allowed to keep running the community garden and given the go-ahead to start my ranch for disadvantaged youth, Ash McDonough comes along as an equal partner in the project."

Maura didn't care that she sounded as imperious as any royal—or that getting Ash to come back to Rumor might be an impossibility, especially if he felt she was once again trying to fix things for him. She couldn't let a detail like that bother her right now.

"I'd even go so far as to say that Ash's involvement is crucial to the ranch's success," she went on. "Because what person could set a better example for troubled kids than someone like Ash, who's been there, paid the price and grown into a good man?"

Her speech done, Maura felt suddenly drained. Her legs were shaking so badly she didn't know if she could remain standing. Yet in the next moment she was sinking into her chair whether she wanted to or not.

An electrified murmur went through the crowd. Maura turned toward the doorway—and she found herself staring at none other than Ash himself.

Ash might have grown roots for all his ability to move. Every face in the room was turned toward him. And every one of them was curious. He couldn't help but think it was because they were wondering what the bad seed of Rumor would do next.

So what would he do? What *should* he do, after hearing Maura's fervent defense of him, even after all that had happened between them today? He couldn't tell, from the faces of the members of the development group, whether she had convinced them to throw off ten years of prejudice against him and endorse her plan—or if she'd effectively cast the die in the other direction.

He had to believe it was the latter. And if so, how could he salvage the situation for her?

He couldn't fail her! That Maura's future happiness rested on his shoulders just about gave him a spontaneous ulcer.

Dammit, how had he let Stratton Kingsley talk him into coming?

But Ash knew how. Maura's father hadn't become one of the most successful businessmen in Montana without some pretty effective negotiation skills.

Ash had been washing off the worst of the fire's damage in his bathroom sink before he started packing, when he'd heard a knock at his apartment door.

Towel in hand, he'd opened the door to find Stratton standing on his narrow stoop.

The rancher had given Ash's soot-stained work shirt and jeans a quick once-over, and from the thin frown on Stratton's face Ash guessed he'd come up lacking— again.

Then Stratton had shrugged. "Well, I guess no one can accuse you of being afraid to get your hands dirty."

He'd brushed past Ash to step into the apartment without invitation. "By the by, that was fine work you did today, saving the Reingard boy."

"Thanks," Ash had said, puzzled and wary as all get-out. "You wanted something, Stratton, besides to pay your first-ever compliment to me?"

"Yeah." Stratton had chucked a thumb over his shoulder. "There's a hearing going on tonight at the library, and you're coming to it, as my guest."

The way he said it, however, it sounded more like a command. And Ash had been feeling perverse enough to take issue with such a tone.

"I'll allow that attending a gathering of your closest friends so's they can take potshots at me does sound like a little slice of heaven on earth, and I'd be delighted as hell to take you up on your kind offer any other time, Stratton,'' he'd drawled. ''But right now I've got an urgent date with a bunch of moving boxes.''

The older man's ears turned a deep shade of red and looked as if steam would come shooting out of them in the next instant. Yet Stratton said civilly, ''All right, I'll let that one slide. But that's the last crack you get for the rest of the year.''

He crammed his fists into the pockets of his trousers and made a production of perusing Ash's meager furnishings: a worn, upholstered armchair, a lamp on a wood veneer side table, a third-hand TV perched on top of a two-by-six stretched across two cinder blocks. It certainly didn't look like the kind of home a father envisioned for his daughter.

Ash wasn't about to apologize. He'd devoted the past five years to putting every penny he could spare toward his dream.

''I do have one question for you, cowboy,'' Stratton finally said, ''and if you never do another honest thing in your life, answer me truthfully.'' He hit Ash with the full force of his gaze. ''Do you love my daughter?''

It was the last thing Ash expected to come out of Stratton Kingsley's mouth. ''Beg pardon?'' he asked, doubting his hearing.

''I asked if you love Maura,'' he repeated impatiently.

Ash hesitated.

''Come on, man! If you've got to think about it—''

''Yes,'' Ash interrupted. He faced Stratton squarely.

"I love your daughter more than I can say. Why do you want to know?"

"Because if you do, you'd better fight for her like you fought for her life in that forest fire." Stratton flung out an arm, pointing east. "The way I guarantee you she's fighting for you as we speak."

Ash crumpled the towel in his hand. "I would if I could see the good it'd do either of us," he said with scant patience. "But just like I told Maura last night, I won't allow her to be dragged down by my reputation any more than I'd allow her to give me a leg up with hers."

He slung the towel onto the armchair, where it landed in a heap. "I couldn't live with myself if I did."

Stratton's mouth drew into a thin line as he regarded Ash, who gazed at the rancher unwaveringly. The older man seemed to be torn—about what, Ash couldn't have said. He sensed, though, that Stratton hadn't wanted to come there and was finding it difficult not to say to hell with it and leave.

But he obviously had a compelling reason to stay.

Finally, he gave a huff and shook his head. "Well, I guess if it's truth or consequences time, I'll go for truth, too," Stratton said. "You wanna know why I've been holding on to the lease for the widow's land? It's so I'd have something to tempt Maura with, to get her to stay around Rumor, like with her ranch for troubled kids."

"Tempt her to stay? You honestly think she'd leave her family?" Ash asked.

"She's done it before, packing off to Missoula when

she was barely old enough to drive, taking up firefighting and gallivanting off to save the forest.''

His lower lip jutted thoughtfully. ''My boys, y'see— none of them have the kind of wanderlust I saw in Maura. It's not in them to leave Rumor, even for love of a woman. Their women would, for love of them, come here. But Maura's mother up and left her family out east to make her life with me, and Maura's a lot like Carolyn that way.''

Chin against his chest, he took an aimless turn around the room. ''So I planned on holding on to that land in case I was lucky enough that the man Maura married would find such a prime piece of Montana grazing land tempting, too, and I'd be able to keep her near her family. I'd like to believe Maura wouldn't be happy anywhere else but here. But she'll make her home where her heart is.''

Stratton had stopped in front of Ash, again giving him a stern eye. ''And like it or not, Ash, you've got her heart. Every bit of it.''

And she has every bit of mine, Ash had thought desolately.

''I don't want to hurt her,'' he'd told Stratton hoarsely. ''I've hurt so many of the people I care about with the mistakes I've made.''

''And you've redeemed yourself.'' The older man had looked at him with surprising benevolence. ''So don't be the rogue people believe you to be and throw Maura's love away. Even with a drug and assault conviction in your past, *that* would be the worst mistake of your life.''

And so Ash had come to the hearing.

He was dislodged from his temporary paralysis by a hand clapped on his shoulder.

"'Scuse me, Ash, but you've got a couple of people who'd like to get inside for the hearing."

He turned to find Colby Holmes behind him, and behind Colby, Max Cantrell, Michael's father.

"Sorry I'm late," Max told Stratton, who stood beside Ash. "I didn't get your cell phone message till I got home from work, then Michael needed some of my time."

"What're you doin' here, Colby?" Ash asked his boss.

The rancher only smiled cryptically. "Let's just say the good old rumor mill's been hard at work again. This time, though, it's been to spread the word about the straits one of our own is in."

He and Max brushed past Ash to take the last two remaining seats.

Willard eyed them suspiciously for a brief moment, then directed his attention to Maura.

"That was quite a speech, young lady," he told her. "And I see that Ash McDonough hasn't quite quit Rumor like he said he would. I can't say as I see that development as being in your favor, since I'm with Dodge on this—funding your ranch project has got to be contingent on the fact that McDonough is nowhere near you, or it."

I knew it, Ash thought with a sinking heart. He'd come here fired up with the conviction of his love for Maura, but nothing had changed since this afternoon. Since he'd returned to Rumor, actually: he was still the bad seed that would contaminate everyone and everything around him.

But when he opened his mouth to assure the panel he was indeed history so far as Maura and Rumor were concerned, another voice preempted his.

"You sure you want to take that stance, Willard?"

Amazingly, the question had come from Reed Kingsley.

The rugged fire chief, still wearing his uniform, had risen to his feet. "I came because DeeDee Reingard pretty much ordered me here, since she had to stay with her son, Parker, while he was being treated for injuries he got in a fire at the Reingard home this afternoon. She said I needed to give you all an accounting of just what contributions Ash McDonough has made. And I gotta say I share my sister's surprise at the attitude some of you have toward Ash, even though I don't really know him, having been on the Rumor fire on and off for the past ten weeks."

There was a murmur of appreciation for such valor.

"A fire, in fact," Reed pointed out, "that Maura contributed her efforts to, as did Ash McDonough who, as I understand it, saved her life in the midst of one of the worst firestorms the crews encountered."

He gave Ash a nod. "I didn't have the chance to say it before, but you've earned my eternal thanks and respect for that."

Ash could only nod back, firefighter to firefighter.

"Anyway," Reed went on, "I don't need to have personal acquaintance with Ash, because I had the opportunity to see him in action today, and again it was in the line of saving a life—Parker Reingard's. And I guess what I'd like to say is, the kind of grit it takes to charge into a burning house with little protection other than the clothes on your back...well, it's hard not to believe that such courage provides more of a measure of who a man is than who he might've been ten years ago.''

There was barely a whisper of either agreement or dispute before another in the room rose to speak.

"I'd also like to say a word in support of Ash McDonough," Max Cantrell said. "Everyone knows what my son Michael and I have been through in the past few months, having my brother Guy go missing and accused of murder. You also know how Michael's had some trouble dealing with those developments.''

He clenched his teeth, his jaw bulging with the effort. "Well, he came to me right before this meeting and said we needed to give Ash the benefit of the doubt. Michael said he could only talk about part of his reason, that being how Ash has been one person he could talk to down at the garden. But he assured me that Maura and Parker Reingard are only two of the people whose lives Ash has saved.''

Colby Holmes stood as Max resumed his seat. "I'd be remiss if I didn't put in a good word for Ash, too.''

He looked at Ash with faint accusation. "I didn't know today when you gave me notice that this was the reason. I'm glad Stratton gave me a heads-up so I could be here.''

He faced the panel again. "Anyway, Ash has worked for me these past few months, and I've got to tell you, there's not a more conscientious, more honest, more hardworking cowboy than Ash McDonough. I think it says enough about how strongly I feel that I made him my right-hand man. And if you don't want to go just by my say-so, I'll get my cousin Dev and my dad to say the same.''

Ash was stunned. If someone had told him he'd have encountered this kind of support here tonight, he'd have called them ten kinds of crazy. It moved him, incredibly so.

Then his gaze encountered Maura's, and he realized that, indeed, *she* had tried to tell him exactly that. And he *had* called her…well, not crazy, but the Montana version of a cockeyed optimist.

She grinned at him in an *I told you so* of the most heartening fashion.

Then Stratton nudged him in the ribs. ''I'd say it's finally your turn to speak,'' he drawled in Ash's ear. ''But you'd better get up there quick, 'fore the rest of your fan club starts in. Jilly's making motions.''

But Ash needed no urging, the force that had rooted him to the floor disappearing.

He walked to the front of the room, coming to a stop to the right of Maura's chair and facing the panel, his Stetson clasped in his hand at his side.

Ash was aware of Maura's closeness, of how much he did not want to let her down. Of how much he loved her.

He couldn't look at her. Not until he'd said his piece.

''Okay, you all have heard a lot about me, which you can take how you wish.'' He was surprised and glad that there was actually some oomph in his voice. ''But not enough's been said about the woman whose dream is in danger of going up in smoke due to her association with me."

He shifted on his feet. The brim of his Stetson was going to be so mangled from his grip on it he feared it'd never straighten out. "Now, I know my credibility factor with most the people in this town is somewhere below zero, but if you never believe anything else, believe this—you'd be daft in the head not to give Maura responsibility for the community garden and the ranch for kids. You'd be depriving every single one of those little souls of the kind of unconditional acceptance and love that doesn't come often enough in this life. But when it does, man—" he blew out a gust of air "—it's life changing."

He stabbed a thumb at his chest. "I know. I'm one of those souls. And I'm tellin' you, if this woman can put *my* broken spirit back together, she can restore that of any child, woman or man."

He couldn't tell from the expressions on the faces of the men in front of him whether he was making an impression, good or bad. He couldn't let that stop him from saying what he had to.

So finally Ash faced Maura. Her blue eyes shone up at him, the tears in them making them shimmer all the more. He gave back as good as he got.

"I love you, Maura," Ash said roughly. "I want more than life to be the man you believe me to be. I know I took the long way around to realizing that, but I promise on my mother's grave I won't stop trying till I am."

She smiled at him, and it was like angels singing.

"You already are that man, Ash," she told him softly. "You always have been."

Then they were in each other's arms. And he was kissing her—her cheeks, her eyes, her mouth. He couldn't get enough of her. He was willing to spend a lifetime trying.

Ash was vaguely aware of a commotion in the room, and it was only when laughter bubbled from Maura's lips as they were pressed against his that he lifted his head. She was smiling and crying at once.

"Did you hear that?" she said. "The development group just voted to fund the ranch. *Our* ranch. Oh, it'll be wonderful, Ash, like a dream come true."

Something made him look up, and over her head Ash saw Stratton, who stood a few yards away with his arm around Carolyn's waist. The two men's gazes met and held.

The rancher nodded. Ash knew it was as much of a blessing as he'd ever get. It was all the blessing that he needed.

"It *is* a dream come true," he said to Maura, gathering her closer. "A dream that I'm hoping will include as many children in need as we can fit in."

Tenderly, he framed her heart-shaped face with his hands. "And I hope as many children of our own that we can handle."

A glow lit her from within. "I can barely believe it," she teased. "Did I really, *really* just hear the H-word come from Ash McDonough's own mouth?"

"Yeah, powder puff," he said with fond tolerance, "you really, *really* did."

And he drew her to him again in a stirring kiss that he hoped would go on forever.

For yes, it *was* hope that filled him, Ash thought, the hope that sprang from the redeeming power of this woman's love…and his love for her.

Like a phoenix it was miraculously rising from the ashes of his heart.

*   *   *   *   *

Don't miss the continuation of

Montana Mavericks: The Kingsleys
*where nothing is as it seems beneath
the big skies of Montana.*

HER MONTANA MILLIONAIRE
by Crystal Green
Silhouette Special Edition 1574

Available November 2003

SWEET TALK
by Jackie Merritt
Silhouette Special Edition 1580

Available December 2003

Coming soon from

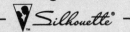
Silhouette®

SPECIAL EDITION™

MONTANA MAVERICKS

THE KINGSLEYS
Nothing is as it seems beneath
the big skies of Montana.

DOUBLE DESTINY

including two full-length stories: FIRST LOVE by Crystal Green
and SECOND CHANCE by Judy Duarte
Silhouette Books
Available July 2003

Moon Over Montana by JACKIE MERRITT
Available July 2003 (SE #1550)

Marry Me...Again by CHERYL ST.JOHN
Available August 2003 (SE #1558)

Big Sky Baby by JUDY DUARTE
Available September 2003 (SE #1563)

The Rancher's Daughter by JODI O'DONNELL
Available October 2003 (SE #1568)

Her Montana Millionaire by CRYSTAL GREEN
Available November 2003 (SE #1574)

Sweet Talk by JACKIE MERRITT
Available December 2003 (SE #1580)

*Available at your favorite retail outlet.
Only from Silhouette Books!*

Silhouette®
Where love comes alive™

Your opinion is important to us! Please take a few moments to share your thoughts with us about your experiences with Harlequin and Silhouette books. Your comments will be very useful in ensuring that we deliver books you love to read. *Please take a few minutes to complete the questionnaire, then send it to us at the address below.*

Send your completed questionnaires to:
Harlequin/Silhouette Reader Survey, P.O. Box 9046, Buffalo, NY 14269-9046

1. As you may know, there are many different lines under the Harlequin and Silhouette brands. Each of the lines is listed below. Please check the box that most represents your reading habit for each line.

Line	Currently read this line	Do not read this line	Not sure if I read this line
Harlequin American Romance	❑	❑	❑
Harlequin Duets	❑	❑	❑
Harlequin Romance	❑	❑	❑
Harlequin Historicals	❑	❑	❑
Harlequin Superromance	❑	❑	❑
Harlequin Intrigue	❑	❑	❑
Harlequin Presents	❑	❑	❑
Harlequin Temptation	❑	❑	❑
Harlequin Blaze	❑	❑	❑
Silhouette Special Edition	❑	❑	❑
Silhouette Romance	❑	❑	❑
Silhouette Intimate Moments	❑	❑	❑
Silhouette Desire	❑	❑	❑

2. Which of the following best describes why you bought *this book?* One answer only, please.

the picture on the cover	❑	the title	❑
the author	❑	the line is one I read often	❑
part of a miniseries	❑	saw an ad in another book	❑
saw an ad in a magazine/newsletter	❑	a friend told me about it	❑
I borrowed/was given this book	❑	other: _____	❑

3. Where did you buy *this book?* One answer only, please.

at Barnes & Noble	❑	at a grocery store	❑
at Waldenbooks	❑	at a drugstore	❑
at Borders	❑	on eHarlequin.com Web site	❑
at another bookstore	❑	from another Web site	❑
at Wal-Mart	❑	Harlequin/Silhouette Reader	❑
at Target	❑	Service/through the mail	
at Kmart	❑	used books from anywhere	❑
at another department store or mass merchandiser	❑	I borrowed/was given this book	❑

4. On average, how many Harlequin and Silhouette books do you buy at one time?

I buy _____ books at one time	❑
I rarely buy a book	❑

MRQ403SSE-1A

5. How many times per month do you shop for any *Harlequin and/or Silhouette* books?
One answer only, please.

1 or more times a week	❑	a few times per year	❑
1 to 3 times per month	❑	less often than once a year	❑
1 to 2 times every 3 months	❑	never	❑

6. When you think of your ideal heroine, which *one* statement describes her the best?
One answer only, please.

She's a woman who is strong-willed	❑	She's a desirable woman	❑
She's a woman who is needed by others	❑	She's a powerful woman	❑
She's a woman who is taken care of	❑	She's a passionate woman	❑
She's an adventurous woman	❑	She's a sensitive woman	❑

7. The following statements describe types or genres of books that you may be
interested in reading. Pick *up to 2 types* of books that you are most interested in.

I like to read about truly romantic relationships	❑
I like to read stories that are sexy romances	❑
I like to read romantic comedies	❑
I like to read a romantic mystery/suspense	❑
I like to read about romantic adventures	❑
I like to read romance stories that involve family	❑
I like to read about a romance in times or places that I have never seen	❑
Other: _____	❑

*The following questions help us to group your answers with those readers who are
similar to you. Your answers will remain confidential.*

8. Please record your year of birth below.

19 _____

9. What is your marital status?

single	❑	married	❑	common-law	❑	widowed	❑
divorced/separated	❑						

10. Do you have children 18 years of age or younger currently living at home?

yes ❑   no ❑

11. Which of the following best describes your employment status?

employed full-time or part-time	❑	homemaker	❑	student	❑
retired	❑	unemployed	❑		

12. Do you have access to the Internet from either home or work?

yes ❑   no ❑

13. Have you ever visited eHarlequin.com?

yes ❑   no ❑

14. What state do you live in?

_____

15. Are you a member of Harlequin/Silhouette Reader Service?

yes ❑   Account # _____   no ❑   MRQ403SSE-1B

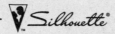

SPECIAL EDITION®

COMING NEXT MONTH

#1573 A LITTLE BIT PREGNANT—Susan Mallery
Readers' Ring
Security expert Zane Rankin could have any woman he wanted…
and often did. Computer hacker and wallflower Nicki Beauman
had contented herself with being platonic with her sexy friend Zane.
Until one night of unbridled—and unexpected—passion changed
their relationship forever….

#1574 HER MONTANA MILLIONAIRE—Crystal Green
Montana Mavericks: The Kingsleys
Sunday driving through life was billionaire and single dad
Max Cantrell's way. Celebrity biographer Jinni Fairchild preferred
living in the fast lane. But when these two opposites collided, there
was nothing but sparks! Could they overcome the detours keeping
them apart?

#1575 PRINCE OF THE CITY—Nikki Benjamin
Manhattan Multiples
When the city's mayor threatened to sever funds for Eloise Vale's
nonprofit organization, she reacted like a mama bear protecting her
cubs. But mayor Bill Harper was her one-time love. Eloise would
fight for Manhattan Multiples, but could she resist the lure of her
sophisticated ex and protect herself from falling for her enemy?

#1576 MAN IN THE MIST—Annette Broadrick
Secret Sisters
Gregory Dumas was searching for a client's long-lost family—
he'd long ago given up looking for love. But in chaste beauty
Fiona MacDonald he found both. Would this wary P.I. give in
to the feelings Fiona evoked? Or run from the heartache he was
certain would follow…?

#1577 THE CHRISTMAS FEAST—Peggy Webb
Dependable had never described Jolie "Kat" Coltrane. But zany and
carefree Kat showed her family she was a responsible adult by
cooking Christmas dinner—with the help of one unlikely holiday
guest. Lancelot Estes, a hardened undercover agent, was charmed
by the artless Kat…and soon the two were cooking up more than
dinner!

#1578 A MOTHER'S REFLECTION—Elissa Ambrose
Drama teacher Rachel Hartwell's latest role would be her most
important yet: befriending her biological daughter. When Rachel
learned that the baby she'd given up for adoption years ago had lost
her adoptive mother, she vowed to become a part of her daughter's
life. But did that include falling in love with Adam Wessler—her
child's adoptive father?